MOURLONET ROSE

Rivara Fall

Mourlonet Rose
Rivara Fall

Mourlonet Rose

Printed in the United States of America

Paperback ISBN: 979-8-9899296-3-4
Hardcover ISBN: 979-8-9899296-4-1
Ebook ISBN: 979-8-9899296-5-8

Edited by: Katie Bucklein
Cover art by: Rivara Fall
Author Website: rivarafall.com

Chapter 1

I wasn't sure why I was staring at a goat. A very still goat... His eyes were a light copper color, and his fur was dark brown with black and tan accents. As far as I could tell, he was just an ordinary goat, standing in front of a mansion, staring at me. It was a little off-putting. I'm sure I would have been more excited walking up to this grand place, ready for an interesting day if she was still with me...and the goat wasn't being so weird. *Has he even blinked? Why does it feel like he's judging me... This has got to be the strangest staring competition I've ever been in.*

The wind picked up, knocking a small red rose onto the ground between us. He bolted off toward a field of horses. Their hooves clamored over the ground as they raced along the fence. *Calm down. I shouldn't... I wasn't there...*

"You alright?" Rodger asked, straightening his tie.

"Nervous." *Just don't think about it.*

"She isn't that bad. About your age, I believe. Try to cheer up. You want to make a good first impression."

The door slowly creaked open, revealing a woman with blonde hair and bright blue eyes. She wore a simple brown and white dress with a flower pattern sewn into the band around the waist.

Rodger tipped his hat. "Evening, Lucinda. We are here to speak with Lady Lorena. She should be expecting us."

The woman smiled and gestured for us to enter. "She's in the lounge."

Glad to be out of the cold. Seems like a nice place. Dark walls, fancy trim, shiny handles on all the doors, extra elegant décor. Makes me feel a bit out of place. I wonder what this lady is going to...

My eyes were immediately drawn to a woman sitting in the lounge on a bright red couch. A simple grey dress and a red jewel necklace offset her pale skin and striking black hair. She was beautiful, though her eyes were the most captivating, grabbing my attention with the type of calm confidence that could stop a raging bull. I'd heard rumors of her family's famous stoic glance. Their nearly black eyes wielded confidence with every look. This was the first time I'd ever actually thought about my posture or my expression. It felt like every inch of the room was watching me. Every surface screamed for my attention. Amongst the hand-carved stone fireplace and the elegant tables and chairs, she fit right in.

Rodger smiled. "Lady Lorena, thank you for seeing us."

Be bold. Just think, what would Viv do? Never mind, I'd rather stay out of trouble.

Lorena sipped her tea. "Your name, dear?"

I sat down. "Eleanora Wintello."

"How long was your family in the wine business?"

"Three generations."

"Did you grow your own grapes?"

"Yes, Carménère."

She reached toward a side table and picked up a simple green bottle with a white logo. *Wintello vino.* "A fair fruit flavor, though I do prefer sparkling beverages, myself. We grow Pinot Noir, Pinot Gris, and Sauvignon Blanc. The Noir is especially difficult to perfect."

I nodded. "It needs precise conditions to grow."

"Yes." Her eyes softened for a moment.

Hopefully that means she's done analyzing me...

"Do you care much for politics?" she continued.

"No. My mother did, but I never really paid attention."

"Boring arguments between fools in fancy attire."

Rodger smiled. "Couldn't agree more."

"Have you been well, Rodger?" she asked.

"The last week has been...difficult. Hopefully tonight I'll have one less job on my hands."

"How many more do you have?"

"One more tonight. A boy from the outskirts of town. He's young, should be no problem finding work. The Attlemyers were hoping to hire on a new stable hand."

"You are too generous, Rodger."

"Are you perhaps feeling generous as well, Lorena?"

She paused and sipped her tea. "She can stay."

"Wonderful." He glanced down at his silver pocket watch. "It's getting late. Everything is in order." He gave me an encouraging smile, then turned toward Lady Lorena. "Thank you for your time."

"Good evening, Rodger."

He tipped his hat and walked out the door. Every footstep deepened my anxiety. The last familiar face I had was getting farther and farther away. *Have to do this on my own now...*

Deep calculating eyes grabbed at my attention. I looked back up at Lady Lorena. *Right, sit up and act formal.*

Lucinda sat next to me. "Intimidated?"

"A little..."

"I know, we're just too beautiful to handle," she said in an exaggerated tone. "You can relax now. We don't bite..." She looked at Lorena. "At least I don't."

Not what I was expecting to hear...

"Can I give you a tour? You must see the indoor garden! Josephine and I agreed it's the best room in the house. Mother thinks it's the library, but the plants help liven up the place more..."

"Slow down, Lucinda," Lorena said, standing up. "It's late. Why don't you get her situated? You can introduce her to the others in the morning. I'll see you both tomorrow."

"Goodnight," Lucinda said, watching her walk out. "We'll get that nervousness out of you eventually. Come on." She grabbed my hand and led me down the hall. Dark maroon paint covered the walls accented with fancy black trim. "Tasks are simple: keep the manor clean, assist our lady when needed, and occasionally help in the garden,

4

though you'll probably be spending most of your time in the winery. Any questions?"

"Is the lady always that intimidating?"

"You'll get used to it." She nudged my shoulder. "Especially with how much you like to look at her."

What? Was I staring? "What do you mean?"

"No judgement. She's very pretty."

She is...

"How are you with dogs?"

"Good, I think."

"We have four that guard the grounds. They'll need to meet you so they don't think you're an intruder." She walked up the intricately carved stairs and led me into another lounge. Dark brown and maroon colors covered most of the room with the occasional flare of gold. Four round, wrinkly orange faces turned to glare at me.

Why is there so much staring...? Is every living thing in this house this intimidating?

She grabbed my hand and placed it onto the larger dog's head. "Famille." His scowl turned into a big goofy smile as he energetically rolled over for a belly rub. "This is Bavero. He's a softie."

Hopefully the rest of this household is similarly soft on the inside. "My parents wanted a guard dog for the field, but couldn't agree on the breed."

"These muscular fuzzballs are French mastiffs, or more fancily known as Dogue de Bordeaux. They're a mess, but nothing is more loyal." She stood and wiped the fur from her dress. "Have you had dinner already? Do you need anything?"

"I'm okay. Just tired... Long day."

She smiled and pointed back out the door. "Your room is two doors down on the left. The one with the leaves carved along the bottom. You'll be staying in one of the guest rooms to start out. The workers' quarters are currently being refurbished. Tasks will be assigned in the morning. I'll come get you when it's time to start."

"Thanks."

"Goodnight."

Two doors...leaves... Here it is. It seems like a nice room. Far fancier than what I'm used to. Large bed, desk, wardrobe, and it looks like it has its own little balcony. I opened the simple glass door and stepped out. Cold winds brushed against the colorful courtyard flowers, lifting loose leaves around a large building at the back. *I guess that's the winery, and the fields are just past it. Looks just as fancy as the manor. Hope the workers aren't too snobbish. Rodger said they were all nice. I'll be fine. I'm here. The day is over. Time to sleep and hope tomorrow goes well. I guess I should assume I'm going to be stared at more. Not used to being alone yet. Everyone used to stare at her...* I closed my eyes and took a deep breath. *I guess I should head to bed. Goodnight, Viv.*

Chapter 2

It's quiet... Doesn't feel right... Did Viv...

I opened my eyes, drearily expecting to see Vivienne hiding in her blankets across the room and the sound of donkeys kicking at the barn door, waiting for their breakfast. Silence was there instead, accompanied by a small pink couch smothered in pillows. *Right, the manor...* Sunlight peeked in through the curtains, giving the room a green hue. *It's still early. Is someone knocking?*

Lucinda opened the door. "Sleep well?"

"Not really. New space."

"Have some breakfast before you head to the winery."

"I'm not feeling all that hungry right now."

"Ok, though I will bug you later if you haven't eaten by dinner time."

"Fair enough." *Better get up and get ready. I've got more adjusting to do.*

-

Another fancy building with a fancy door, though this one has leaves carved on it and metal grape vines around the arch. At least I'm not getting stared at again... Never mind, there's a goat peaking around the corner. Is it the same one?

"Pete!" a woman yelled, causing him to bolt out of sight.

Viv would have probably chased after him to see what's going on. It's still too quiet without her.

The door opened, revealing a skinny gentleman with dark brown skin, roughly my height. He wore tan boots, a new pair of brown working pants, and a dark red shirt. "You must be Eleanora," he said. "My name is Anthony. You ever worked in a vineyard before?"

"Family business. Carménère grapes."

"Then I assume you know your way around the barrels. We have a fairly chaotic system, but we get it done."

"I should be fine."

"Come on in. Take a look. We have three main rooms, one for storing and processing the grapes, one for barrel storage, and one for bottling. We have quite a few field workers, but you'll mostly work with myself, Gerome, and Frolont. Gerome is that skinny old man in the corner."

"I ain't old," Gerome said with a smile.

"You're practically dust."

"I'm thirty-six."

"Then why are you always so dusty?"

"I get things done around here. Someone's got to pick up the slack Frolont leaves."

"Frolont doesn't spend as much time in the bottling room. Watching him take a swig of wine, then fumble around shelves full of glass is a nightmare. It's better to just let him sit on top his little truck outside and complain the day away."

"Grumpy supervisor sort?" I asked.

"Exactly," Anthony answered.

Gerome reached out and took my hand. "Elenora, right?"

"Yes."

"Good to have another face around here. I've been staring at Anthony's for too long."

Anthony threw a rag at him. "You know I'm handsome."

"Compared to this?" Gerome gestured at himself. "Can't beat this look."

"Anyone could."

"Says the man who wears his work clothes everywhere."

"They're comfortable and durable."

"Take your wife out to dinner in those clothes one more time and I'll shove you into a suit myself."

"I'll wear one the day Frolont stops drinking."

"If that happens, I'll wear one too."

"Speaking of Frolont," Anthony said, turning back toward me. "We'd better introduce you. Just keep quiet and do what he says. You shouldn't have to interact with him too much." He opened a smaller wooden door, letting the cool wind rush in.

There's so many grapes. They look healthy. These people know what they're doing.

"Frolont is in charge of production," Anthony said, leading me up the muddy hill. "He makes sure everything is precise. He can be...a little stern."

I'm guessing the angry looking man standing on the back of that truck is him. His glaring is a lot scarier than Lorena's.

"You're the Wintello girl?" Frolont asked, hopping down off the truck bed.

"Yes."

He narrowed his eyes and frowned. "Carménère grapes are basic. No originality. I won't touch them. My skills are fine-tuned for true elegance. I don't know why the lady wants you here. You probably can't tell the difference between the Blanc and Gris. Huh, no matter. You're here now, so we might as well get on with it. Assign her something, Anthony. I'm busy."

"Of course." Anthony turned, rolled his eyes, then led me back to the building.

This is more familiar, though their fields are far larger and better maintained. The blunt remarks of workers, the cold clang of bottles, and the chill breeze that rushes by every now and then knocking more and more leaves off the vines is much easier to deal with than getting stared at by a distractingly beautiful woman and her buff guard dogs.

10

"I assume you've met Lorena. What do you think?" Anthony asked, opening the door.

"She's a bit intimidating."

"She's not that bad. Doesn't lash out like Frolont. You don't have anything to worry about."

Except how pretty she is.

He walked up to a shiny bottling machine and began messing with the round center piece that moved the bottles. "Nothing like working with a broken machine right before progress reports are due."

I stepped closer, examining its structure. *Looks much nicer than the one we had. Ours was just a simple five bottle filling machine. This one's got a fancy turntable and a capping function.* "What should I get started on?"

"Go help Gerome dust off the bottles in the back room over there. Once I'm done, we'll get back to bottling."

This is a cool room. Fancy brick archways with old stained wooden shelves full of bottles.

Gerome carefully set a bottle back onto the shelf and turned toward me. "Here to help?"

"Yes."

"There's another duster by the door. These bottles are private stock, reserved for events and fancy meetings."

"What do we make?"

"We make four main types of wine. Mourlonet Noir, Mourlonet Blanc, Mourlonet Sanguine, and Mourlonet Rose. The Sanguine is our most widely sold. Dark red with the perfect balance of sweet and sour. The Rose is more delicate and aromatic. It's infused with rose petals handpicked from the property. We only make a few batches of this per season. One of the rarest."

"They really like their last name."

"Yep. Our more widely available wines are made with crushers, while the Rose and Sanguine are made traditionally. Play some good music on the radio and dance like mad men."

"Mother forbade us from dancing on the grapes. She always thought we'd make a mess."

He smiled. "Takes longer but keeps us fit."

"What about that back shelf? Those all have different labels."

"Lord Percival was passionate about collecting different wines from all over the world. Some of those are worth a fortune, including the old families' bottles."

"Old families?"

"The red bottles with the gold and white logo of a wine bottle surrounded by a ring of grape leaves were made by the famed Mourellio wine makers based in Italy. A number of generations back, they married into the Elonet family. A powerful French family famed for their wines. They made those clear bottles with the red horse on the front. When the families joined, they combined the name to make Mourlonet and became one of the most respected families in the winemaking business."

"Interesting."

"You will hear both French and Italian while you're here. Do you know either?"

"I was raised on both English and Italian."

"Good, you shouldn't get too lost. How long has your family been here?"

"My grandfather moved out here to start a new business in wine. He still primarily spoke Italian. Made sure my parents, my sister, and myself were fluent."

"Right, you're from the Wintello family." He picked a green bottle off the shelf. "Lorena bought those the day Rodger called. They'll be worth a fortune a few years from now."

Our wine... That's one of the last bottles we made. I remember sitting on the bench, listening to Vivienne complain about boredom. We had spent the whole week before the fair bottling and getting ready for sales.

"I haven't tried it," Gerome continued. "I don't drink often. Heard it's good."

"I wonder what it would be like if our wine had ended up getting popular. If I ended up as a competitor rather than a worker. Grandfather was certain we would be famous one day."

"Well, I would have to dust these bottles alone for one thing."

I glanced back down at the bottle in my hand. "I used to get sick of staring at this green glass all day... I grew up staring at these bottles, cleaning them off, and filling them up. Grandad would always look at them and smile. He

13

always wanted to be known for something. Seeing his name on the bottles made him feel accomplished. He would show them off to all his friends and brag about his success, even though we weren't all that successful."

"Is he still around?"

"No. He died a few years ago."

"Well, I'm sure he'll be smiling when those sell for hundreds a piece. Even small company wine is valuable when it becomes rare enough. Especially to collectors."

"Yeah..." *I'm sorry grandad. I couldn't keep up the company on my own. Hope you aren't disappointed.*

Chapter 3

I closed the winery door and took a deep breath. *Update on the goat backstory, Viv. He seems to have something against Gerome. Though honestly, if a man ran away from me, flailing and whining like a child, I would probably enjoy chasing him around, too. I'm sure you would have found it all entertaining—hell, you probably would have cheered the goat on.*

The sound of hooves and excited chuffs pulled my attention toward the barn. Lorena sat atop a large black horse as he trotted along the fence. She was wearing professional black pants, a long-sleeved maroon shirt, and shiny black boots. *She looks so elegant, commanding his movements with a gentle hand. He seems to have noticed me. He's kicking his legs higher and holding his head up more... Is he trying to show off?*

The pair stopped next to me. "Evening, Elenora."

"Lady Lorena."

"Just Lorena, dear."

"What's his name?" I asked, petting the horse's head.

"Arkello."

"He seems energetic."

"He is. Smart, determined, and precise. I've honestly never seen a horse more excited to learn a new task."

"And excited to show off?"

She smiled. "Always. How did your day go?"

"It was interesting. Anthony and I spent the morning watching Gerome get chased around by a goat. After that, we finished packaging the private buyer crates."

"Sounds entertaining."

"Very. It's nice how relaxed everything is. I honestly thought it would be more...strict working here."

"People tend to be more productive if you aren't shoving them toward their tasks."

"Thank you, again, for letting me stay."

"Have you been given any further tasks for the evening?"

"No. Is there anything you need me to do?"

"You're welcome to keep me company, if you'd like. I was originally hoping to catch the show tonight, but I ended up caught up in paperwork. Thought a ride would help me relax."

"Show?"

"The theatre in Canterfollo is premiering a new show tonight. I was hoping to be done in time to catch the train."

"Which show was it?"

"*Along the Red Horizon.* I believe it's a dramatic opera. I've been talking with the mayor about getting a theatre built in town. My parents set aside funds to support its construction."

"Do you go to the theatre often?"

"I try, though it has been difficult lately. Have you seen many shows?"

"Just one. *The Follies of the Ocean King.* It was a few towns away. Dad let us join him on one of his business trips. One of the most stunning buildings I'd ever been in. It was painted dark turquoise with gold and white accents, and the ceiling was covered in a large floral mural. The show was very dramatic and loud, and maybe went a little extra with the flashing lights."

"What was it about?"

"A lonely king lost his son to the sea and would go out to the docks every night to sing to his spirit. The sirens heard his sorrowful cries and decided to return his son to him in exchange for his crown. The man tossed it into the sea, and his son swam to shore. I liked it, but my mother didn't care for the theatre. She was worried that we would get too excited and try to run off to become actresses. To be fair, my sister might have."

"My mother would take us to every new show. She liked to use it as a learning opportunity, told us to pay attention to their voices, their posture, the way the music shifts and flows."

"We were told to watch how all the farming chores were done, though I also had to listen to a fair amount of singing. The donkeys tried, at least..."

She smiled and looked into my eyes. Again, it felt like they were thoroughly examining me. Every second felt like I was being dissected and put in my place, though I still felt a sense of understanding. The fancy buildings and perfectly maintained flowers around me screamed for proper etiquette and respect, but every time I was next to her over the past couple weeks, every expectation and concern faded. I would occasionally have to remind myself that she was noble. The thought always pulled me a little farther away and made me less talkative. She always seemed to notice.

"Are you getting along with everyone?" she asked.

"Yes."

"I know some of them can be a bit much sometimes."

"Frolont is loud, but not too bad. Anthony and Gerome are really nice, and Lucinda is energetic, but I like the energy. It's familiar..." *Vivienne...*

"Do you want to elaborate?" she asked.

Those eyes again, staring with curiosity, maybe concern? I'm not fluent in Lorena's looks. She doesn't seem to be the most expressive person. "Not right now."

"Ok."

It didn't always hurt. It was better when I kept myself busy, but every time I'd notice the quiet, the lack of her presence, everything would slow. I'd get colder; lose my focus. I'd smile at the good memories, then get hit with a wave of chilled depression as I recalled the first night I'd spent alone.

"There's nothing you could have done... I'm sorry, truly."

18

I could still see Rodger standing at the door with a somber expression, one I'd never seen on him. He was always smiling, always helping people out. The man in town that everyone went to for a favor or advice. The man who always wore bright colors, claiming that everything needed vibrance. Seeing him on the front porch in that suit...I knew...

Lorena reached out. "Care for a ride?"

I hesitantly took her hand. "Are you sure?"

"Of course."

I hopped up behind her and awkwardly put my arms around her waist. She jerked the reigns. Arkello galloped forward, flying out the gate, racing past the vines. Workers rushed out of the path. My concern turned into a smile. *What have I gotten myself into?*

We rushed across the top of the hill, watching the sunset shift over the sprawling fields of grapes. The bright colors of the garden contrasted the dark stone walls of the manor. The light green vines and bright pink and red petals from the rose bushes stood out against the dark shadowed leaves and twisted branches of the forest.

Arkello flew past the trees, weaving through them at full speed. Every hoofbeat filled with certainty, like they'd run this route a hundred times. The trail was worn down into a fine line that his hooves never missed.

I closed my eyes, feeling the wind's crisp sting. Odd to think, I was perfectly relaxed while thundering though the woods on a massive horse. Everything else faded into the background. No thoughts, no worries, just the cool breeze, the scent of flowers, and the warmth of another person. Simple... Familiar.

"Vai più veloce!" Vivienne yelled.

The small brown pony quickened his pace across the wooden bridge. Large salmon cluttered the creek below, splashing up at us. Vivienne turned us down a steep hill, dodging trees and bushes until we jumped out onto the road.

Uncle Max laughed, slowing his horse. "You kids are much wilder than your parents. Your father was always too scared to go any faster than a trot." He dismounted his horse and grabbed the reins. "Bring him to the post. We'll give the horses a break. Should have you back home in time for dinner."

The thundering slowed. I opened my eyes as we approached the barn. My mind took a second to readjust. *Lorena's warmer than Viv.*

"Alright?" she asked, helping me down.

"Yes. It reminded me of the time our uncle would watch us. We always got to ride back home. He had a little pony for Viv and me. I think his name was Sir Gideon. Energetic, though not nearly as much as Arkello."

"I'm glad."

She's still holding my hands. They're warm.

"Most people are afraid to hold on tight."

"Scared of having their hands on a noble?"

"Yes," she said with a sly smile. "You didn't seem as bothered."

"You did invite me."

"Brave enough to go again?"

"Any time."

"Alright." She let go of my hands and led her horse back into the barn.

Out of all the places I could have wound up, I'm standing in a field, mesmerized by a lady far out of my league. This is going to be interesting...

Chapter 4

Lucinda was right. The kitchen has the perfect amount of light for reading. The rustic charm, tan tiled floors, dark wooden cabinets with gold handles, a door at the back, and a window that looks out to the vegetable garden. Feels more comfortable than the overly dressed rest of the house.

"Story or research?"

I set down my coffee mug, turning to see Lorena in the doorway. "Research."

She walked up to me, looking down at the book. "What sort?"

"I thought I should learn more about Pinot Noir. My father talked about it once or twice but never really went into detail, and Mr. Frolont can be a bit..."

"Difficult?"

"Yes. He tried to explain its needs in between complaints and remarks."

"What sort of remarks?"

"Well..."

"I'd like you to be honest with me. Some of the workers have been complaining about his behavior."

"He...hasn't been the friendliest, but he's not being overly offensive."

"Let me know if he crosses any lines."

"He has been drinking during work. I wasn't sure if I should mention it."

"Our bottles?"

"Yes, usually Noir."

"Is he trying to hide it?"

"A little, though I believe most of the other workers know. They just don't really want to cross the man in charge."

"Thank you, El. I'll have Anthony keep an eye on the situation. I trust he has been treating you well?"

"Yes."

"Good. Have you completed your tasks for the day?"

"Yes. Lucinda suggested I read here. Close to snacks and tea, and has the perfect amount of light for reading."

"Could I persuade you to take a break?"

"And do what instead?"

"Michella and I are going on a ride today. You're welcome to join us."

"I'd love to."

She opened the door and stepped out into the sun. *Beautiful in any lighting... Wait, stop, don't let her catch you staring. I wonder if this happens often. She is noble. People probably stare anyways.*

"Michella should be saddling them now," Lorena said, opening the barn door.

Surprised the barn doesn't have horses carved on the doors as well. It's a bit more rustic. Still far nicer than our old barn. Is that Italian music coming from the back? I recognize that song.

A short, tough-looking woman stood next to a large grey horse. "You must be Eleanora, good to see you. I'm Michella. I handle most of the barn work, drive the carriage, and help in the gardens when needed."

"Who do you have here?" I asked, reaching toward the horse.

"Baketrot. We got him from the auction," she said, tying up her scraggly orange hair. "Friend of mine said there was a horse we'd be interested in. Wasn't in great condition, but he had all his paperwork. Great riding horse. Definitely the calmest." She lifted the saddle onto his back with ease. "Will you be joining us?"

"Yes."

"You speak Italian, correct?"

"Yes."

"I'll have you ride Bellezza today. She knows Italian commands. You know how to saddle her up?"

"Yes."

"Good. She's the black one over there sneaking into the barrel of apples. A bit mischievous, but well-behaved."

Bellezza tapped her hooves with excitement as I lifted the saddle onto her back. *Of course she has fancy red roses embroidered on her saddle and reins. Wonder how much this all cost. If only Uncle Max's saddles were as soft as this. I remember being so sore after riding that draft horse he was training. Had the most uncomfortable old saddle.*

"Ready to go?" Michella asked. "We'll go around the north loop today. Lorena will be in the front, you in the middle, and I'll take the rear."

I swung up onto Bellezza and grabbed hold of her reins. *Definitely bigger than Uncle Max's horses... Something's off. She's standing unusually still.* I tightened my grip. *Looks like she's going to...run!*

"Fermare, Bellezza!" Michella yelled, watching her sprint forward.

Oh no... She flew over the fence, racing toward the courtyard. I pulled back on the reins and tried to calm her down. Every command was ignored. Her hooves thundered against the ground. *Don't think about it... I wasn't there... It shouldn't bother me...*

"Look at their movements, their posture, their ears, and head. What are they telling you?"

She's not acting scared...

"Sometimes they just need to run."

I let go of the reins and took a deep breath. The grass swayed beneath us. The setting sun flooded the sky with warmth. She sped up, falling into a smoother rhythm. She shook her head and let out a deep breath. *That's better... Michella and Lorena aren't that far behind. Hopefully Bell stops soon. Try to calm down. She isn't running into anything. The property fence is too tall for her to jump. We'll be okay. Viv and I used to do defiant stuff like this all the time. It's just scary without her.*

25

Bellezza quickened her pace. *Oh no. Why are we bolting straight towards a car? A moving car. Is this horse plotting to end me?* "Please don't."

She let out a huff, then kicked off the ground, flying over the car. *Please don't kill me, please don't kill me. I like it here. Whoa. Okay, it's done. We're still alive.* "Calmati, Bellezza." *She's finally stopping. That was intense.*

"You alright?" Michella asked, catching up.

"Yes, she's listening now."

"I didn't expect her to take off like that."

"When was she last ridden?"

"A month or so. Whenever Lady Lillian took her out last."

"Has anyone else ridden her before?"

"No...now that I think about it."

"Mother used to jump her over the fence to irritate father," Lorena said. "It seems she developed a few bad habits."

"I think she just needed to get out," I said. "Just needed to run."

"At least she didn't leave the property. Think you can get her back to the barn?"

"Yes, we're fine now."

"Good. I'm sure you've had enough excitement for one day."

"Yeah."

"You handled that well."

"Not much I could do besides hold on... My uncle was good at working with difficult horses. He said that sometimes they just need to run."

"Would you be up to riding her again?" Lorena asked. "I think she just needs more work."

"Sure, though I might need some lessons on how to jump properly."

"Michella can teach you. She was Mother's instructor."

Michella laughed. "I'm sure you'd make a far less stubborn student. That woman was something."

Was? Bell stopped and stared at the barn fence. "Oh no... Please don't." *Of course she's jumping over it. First horse I've met that sees every fence as a challenge. I get why her saddle is so soft now. Would be a nightmare jumping in a stiff one.*

"Do you have something against gates?" I said, leading her toward the barn.

Lorena smiled. "She wants to give you a challenge."

"I get enough of those working with Frolont." I got down and began taking off her saddle. "My uncle had us help with the horses when we would visit. He used to rent them out. Had a whole field of them, different sizes and colors, too many names to remember, but he knew each one."

"Is he still around?"

"No, he moved back to Italy a year ago."

"I grew up with two aunts," Lorena said. "One is particular about her horses. She will only pick the perfect crosses, those who have equal Percheron and Lipizzaner characteristics. Have to be the exact right height and shape. Grey in color."

"Did she always give them the same name? Basically picked the same horse over and over again."

"No, but she always called them Sir or Madam. Her current horse is Madam Extravaganza."

"Are they all the same type of cross?" I asked.

"Yes. My family originated from the Mourellio and Elonet families. The Mourellios had beautiful Lipizzaner horses. The Elonets had Percherons, favoring their strength. When the families came together, they decided to combine their strengths. The wine, the horses, and the family name."

"Strength and beauty."

"Something I admire," Lorena said, looking me over with a soft smile.

Is she flirting with me? Probably not... I turned toward Michella as I brushed Bellezza down. "How long have you worked for the family?"

"Twelve years, I think. Used to work at the races as a kid. Was a bit too hectic for me. Much prefer this sort of work, taking care of rich people's animals. Pays good, less drama."

"How many horses do you have here?"

"Nine. Our three here. Then Crowmont. He's the skinny black one out in the field. Then we have Gloris and

Vinyara. They're the large light greys. And we've got Helena and her foals in the barn."

"You have foals?"

"Two. You two can go feed them, if you'd like. I can finish up with these three."

Lorena smiled and took my hand, leading me to a smaller building behind the barn. She tapped her hand on the gate and whistled. A smaller white horse poked her head out of the stall. Two solid black foals darted out into the small pasture. "That's Gellon and Griffin. Only a month old. Incredibly friendly. They will make fine horses one day."

I couldn't help but smile. "My uncle would adopt orphan foals. He had one, only a few days old. The scrawniest little horse I'd ever seen. His legs wiggled and wobbled beneath him, though he didn't seem to notice. He'd still run across his stall to greet my uncle every morning, usually falling into the door. My uncle had to put up a pile of hay behind it to keep him from getting injured."

"They are clumsy things."

"Were all the horses born here?"

"Arkello, Bellezza, and Crowmont were. The grey ones were purchased from a family friend who specializes in Percheron-Lipizzaner crosses. I liked Arkello's energy, his confidence. He acts like nothing in the world could ever restrain him."

"I know someone like that." I glared at her with a playful smile. "Maybe a bit less energetic."

"Self-control is one of the first rules of polite society." She stepped closer. "Though I do have my moments."

"Get the occasional urge to run through the field?"

"Not quite. Perhaps one day I'll take you for a run."

My heartbeat quickened. *She's not actually talking about running, is she? Okay, we're flirting, no big deal... Okay a huge deal. Damn, I wish Viv were here. She'd know what to say...* "I'll go on any adventure with you."

"I'll keep that in mind." Her eyes swept over me in a fairly obvious manner. It reminded me of Viv's lectures. She would often come home late after hanging out with friends and go on and on about social standards, body language, and eye contact. She would lay back in her bed and try to explain different expressions and what they meant. The subtle differences that told entire stories if you knew how to read them.

What are hers telling me?

"Why don't you go inside and relax for a while, El? I'm sure all this excitement has been tiring."

"I'll try, though I assume Luce will want to hear about it."

"You'll need to prepare yourself to be bombarded with questions."

"I'm used to it."

She smiled and turned back toward the barn.

Luce is going to find me the moment I walk in, isn't she? I walked up to the kitchen door and reached for the handle.

"Did she really jump three fences and a car?" Lucinda asked as I pulled it open.

"Yes," I responded.

"I'm surprised you didn't fall off."

"So am I."

"Are they going to retrain her?"

"Michella is going to give me jumping lessons."

"Really? You're not scared?"

"No. It will be good for Bell."

Lucinda grinned. "Brave and good with animals. I'm sure Lorena is impressed."

I threw a towel at her. "Stop."

She threw it back. "Never."

I took a deep breath and sat down at the small table in the corner. "I was a little scared...not because of Bell. Every time I hear clamoring hooves, I can't help but think of it. It started the morning after. I went to take care of the donkeys. They ran out into the pasture and...I just froze. The sound just... I wasn't even there. Why does it bother me so much?"

She took my hands. "Your brain is trying to make sense of it. You didn't see what happened, you were told. It's not as easy to understand from a description, so your brain tries to create it, understand it."

"Thanks." I looked out the window, watching the flowers sway in a gentle breeze. "You are all so wonderful. It's not exactly how I imagined. I guess I expected more stuck-upness and restrictions working for a noble family."

"This family's always been fair to their workers. Most others of high-class aren't as friendly. We have one worker that used to work for the Vintmarkel family. They were atrocious. Lord Mourlonet saw how they treated her and immediately removed her from the house." She paused, looking at the floor. "He was a good man."

"I haven't seen Lorena's parents. Are they…"

"Died in the fair stampede, along with her brother, Lucian."

"Oh…"

"She was beside herself for a few days, distraught with grief. Then you came along. A lonely girl who had just lost everything. You both needed someone. Her attitude returned to normal after you showed up. She had a new interest to distract her."

"I sort of feel the same. Looking at her… Her voice, her smile. Being around someone so elegant and beautiful…"

I noticed a grin appear on her face. "I was right. You're starting to fall for her, aren't you?"

"What?" I looked down. *Am I…* "I…guess I do admire her…"

"Denial," Lucinda accused. "You've been staring with infatuation all week."

"I... Alright. She's noble and stunning. I can't even think about approaching her in any romantic sense."

"I know she's grown fond of you. We'll just have to see how things unravel."

She's...fond of me? I guess she does make comments sometimes, but I wasn't sure if she actually liked me. Viv would be able to tell. I really need to work on my people skills.

Chapter 5

"I'd say we've had enough for the day," Anthony declared, sitting back against a crate. "If I look at one more grape, I'm going to go mad."

"I agree."

"You can head back to the manor if you'd like, El."

"I might wait a bit. The rain is getting crazy."

"You can use the tunnel if you want to stay dry."

"Tunnel?"

"That old door near the entrance connects to a tunnel that leads to the basement of the manor. We typically use it to store extra bottles. Lucinda likes to hide down there and listen in on our conversations."

"Really?"

Lucinda opened the door. "I was going to try and surprise her, Anthony."

"Too late," he said. "You should have told me your plan. That would have been fun."

"You going to head home now, Anthony?"

"Not in this weather. I might just spend the night in the back again."

"As long as you don't start drinking our stuff like Frolont."

"No, I'd rather keep my head screwed on."

"Good luck with that. You ready, El?"

"Yeah. Bye, Anthony." *The tunnel is freezing. At least I'm not getting all wet.*

"Did you have a good day?" Lucinda asked.

"Yeah. We were finally able to get caught up on bottling. One of the machines keeps breaking. Doesn't help that Frolont just insults them. Like that's going to fix a broken piece of metal."

"Well, you're free from all the yelling now. How about I introduce you to a much quieter and kinder person? You haven't met Joey yet, have you?"

"No."

"She was out visiting her family for the past couple weeks. Got back this morning." She led me into the laundry room and walked up to a shorter, chubbier woman with light brown hair and eyes. "This lovely lady is Josephine. Everyone usually calls her Joey. She's our chef's assistant. Occasionally helps me with chores."

Joey smiled. "Glad to meet you. Sorry you have to deal with Frolont. I've never met him, but I know he can be difficult."

Lucinda spoke. "I'd gladly do any house chores rather than spend an hour with him."

"You can at least understand what he's saying," Joey continued. "Not all of us know French."

"True, and I guess he isn't the worst, just likes to insult people."

"Better than my previous employers."

"I told El about the Vintmarkells. Snobbish sexist assholes."

"They were...far worse than him," Joey said with an uneasy expression. "They were awful to all their staff, even the butler who had been there for over thirty years. I can't imagine how they were raised to act like that. They don't even care about reputation, they just like belittling people."

Luce put a hand on her shoulder. "And now they have only two staff members because other nobles keep stealing them away to better homes. Soon they'll have to do all their chores themselves."

Joey smiled. "They would despise that."

"And we would all love to see it."

"I'm just glad to be here now." She turned and opened the dryer. "How about you two help me fold these sheets? There's only a few left."

Luce grabbed a sheet and tossed it onto me dramatically. "You're now an extravagant ghost."

"We'll, we can't have just any ghost haunting this place," I said. "Only the finest silk-covered spirits are acceptable."

"Must be hard to be a ghost in a manor. Having to keep up with fashion standards."

"Does being a ghost mean I don't have to do any more chores?"

"I'm not sure...but if it does, I'm joining you." She tossed another sheet into the air and let it fall onto her.

"Hey," Joey started, "you're just going to leave me to do everything?" She pulled the sheets off us and finished folding. "There, last one is done. Would have gone by faster if you were helping me instead of spying on the winery again."

Luce shrugged. "I wanted to surprise Eleanora, but Anthony ruined it."

Joey looked at the clock. "We have an hour left until I have to go help with dinner. Are there any more chores that need done today?"

"We still have to dust all four-thousand, three-hundred and seventy-nine books in the library."

Joey put her hands on her head. "She made me help count them on one of our days off. I nearly lost my sanity."

"I wanted to know how many we had," Luce said. "Especially after Lady Lillian stated she had read every book in the manor."

"Lady Lillian?" I asked.

"Lorena's mother."

Joey sighed and sat on the couch. "Why don't you go see if Lorena needs anything, El? She just got done with a meeting. Should be in her study. We can handle the books. It honestly doesn't take as long as it sounds."

"Where is her study?"

"Next to the library. The room with the snowy carriage painting."

"Try not to get too distracted by her looks," Luce said with a wink.

"I..." *I do get a little distracted. I really need to fix that. Stop daydreaming and be respectful. She's a noble. She will expect nothing but respect. Let's see, next to the library... Here it is. A cozy room with a desk in the center, bookshelves to the left and a few smaller chairs to the right. There's that snowy carriage painting Luce mentioned. Can't wait to see what this place looks like when it snows. All the fancy brick work, the warm glow of light coming through the curtains. I bet their holiday celebrations are extraordinary.*

Lorena looked up from her papers. "How was your day, El?"

"Busy. We managed to get caught up on bottling. I got to meet Joey. She seems really nice. Not as wild as Luce."

"Every day is another wild adventure with Lucinda."

"Honestly not too different than what I'm used to." I sat across from her. "My sister... She was energetic and wild, too."

"Is it hard having someone similar?"

"Not really. I almost feel like my purpose is to be an accomplice to wild shenanigans. I must be around a troublemaker at all times. Viv and I were inseparable. She was always dragging me around. At least now I'm not alone. Joey seems to just go along with it like I do."

"She's sweet and doesn't mind Luce's energy. They work well together. I'm sure you fit right in."

"I hope."

She smiled and glanced out the window. "Our manor has always been a puzzle. People fitting together like perfectly cut pieces. My parents always had an eye for compatibility, as does Rodger. I knew I could trust his judgement when he brought you here."

"I feel like I fell out of one puzzle and right into another. It's nice having that sense of belonging."

"You are welcome to try out all sorts of places, see the beauty of different situations, different puzzles, and discover the images they make and the stories they tell. If you ever choose to leave, you will always have a place here."

"Thank you." *I'm glad I'll always be welcome here. I can't imagine ever wanting to leave.* "How did your meeting go?"

"They wanted to clarify some contract details that weren't discussed last week. I don't think I've met more business-oriented people."

"Not the best company?"

"The Botligs are arrogant and opinionated, though they have one of the most efficient shipping companies in their name. My father made a contract with them. They were the only ones with access to the eastern railway for a while." She sighed. "I have a few more papers to go over before dinner."

"Do you need any help?"

"How much do you know about profit reviews?"

"Not much. My mother took care of that."

"It used to be my father's job."

"I didn't know about your parents. I'm sorry."

"It is nice to have someone who understands."

"Is that why you let me stay?"

"We were both alone, struck by the same misfortune. You needed a new life, a home. Mine was empty and quiet."

"Thank you."

She smiled. "Would you like to tell me about them?"

"I shared a room with my sister. Whoever woke up first got to throw pillows at the other until they got up. We were in charge of taking care of the animals before breakfast. The donkeys were very commanding. Mother would be in the kitchen swearing about the weather or politics until breakfast was done. Then she would start yelling for our father to come back inside. He would get up before everyone else every morning and go stare at the grapes in complete silence, determining if they were ready or not."

"Just stare at them?"

"Yes. Mother used to tease him about it. He started doing that with his dad when he was a kid. It paid off, he always knew exactly what the vines needed every day. A true grape whisperer."

"Frolont is excellent with vine care, though his methods aren't as quiet."

"At least you always know where he is. Some people thought it was a little odd seeing Dad just standing in the same spot every morning, staring at leaves in silence."

"The quiet, odd ones are often the most intelligent."

"You are proof of that." *That made her smile. She's so beautiful.* "What about your family?"

"My brother Lucian was always the first one up. He liked to join the maids for breakfast so he could steal extra muffins. Father would go straight to the study to look over reports with our advisor. Mother would meet me in the lounge for tea before breakfast. Lucian and I would help with company matters, hone our riding skills, and observe workers in the winery."

"A typical noble upbringing, I assume?"

"Yes. Mother had high expectations and plans for our futures."

"Be good at everything, act professional, and continue the family name?"

"Yes, though we were both stubborn about suitors. Father didn't pressure us. He wanted the best. For him, that meant letting us find our happiness."

"I wasn't really pressured, either."

"Do you have a romantic interest?"

Maybe... Yes... "I was busy with the family business. Vivienne was always the more romantic one. A pro at flirting."

"Really?"

"Quite the charmer."

41

"No doubt, if she was as striking as you."

She is flirting... "She was a little shorter and her hair was a lighter brown, but we had the same green eyes. One of her boyfriends would confuse us when he was drunk."

"Sounds fairly problematic."

"It wasn't too bad. He came over drunk one night when Viv was out. He was so confused when I kept backing away from him. Had a sad expression. Kept asking why I wouldn't kiss him. He laughed at himself and backed off when I reminded him who I was."

"Most noble men are more respectful, though I have had a few who drank too much and became a nuisance. A Spanish nobleman once approached me at a party. He was charming and arrogant, not much different from the rest. He spent a good three hours trying to impress me, and then his wife stormed in and made a scene."

"At least it was entertaining."

"Very." She scribbled her signature on the last page and stood. "Thank you for staying. It goes much faster with company."

"I'll keep you company whenever you need."

"Glad to hear that. I am interested in having someone else assist with company matters. Perhaps you'd be open to learning more about the internal workings of the company? My schedule has been exhausting. Having another hand would make life far easier."

"Of course. Whatever you'd like." *That's a suspicious look... Adorably devious. I wonder what she's thinking.*

42

"Come, let's see what the chef made tonight. He was excitedly rambling earlier about a new shipment from France. That man will cook anything, no matter the challenge."

"Fitting for this household."

Chapter 6

"Is she ever going to slow down?" I asked, leaning closer to Joey.

"No," she responded, continuing to stare as Luce ran around the kitchen, preparing cookie dough.

"Is she at least a good cook?"

"Yes. She's good at pretty much everything, even with how fast she goes."

Luce aggressively stirred the bowl of dough. "Just need to put it into the pan...set it in the oven...then we wait."

"Still amazes me," Joey started. "You were raised by the slowest and most rule-abiding woman on the planet, and yet you race around with unlimited energy. It took almost all day for me and your mother to swap out all the curtains. I spent so long following her around, listening to her mumble about the rugs and the paintings and whatever she thought needed cleaning next. I swear, the woman only thinks about this manor."

Luce spoke. "I love her, but she is slower than that old dog that wanders around town."

"Old Dusty Toes?" I asked.

"Yes. That dog looks and moves like an ancient relic that crawled out of a dusty cave, even after people washed him off."

I smiled. "My sister used to joke around about him being a ghost dog since he looks so grey. No one really knows where he came from. One guy even suggested making him the mayor. Did you vote for him?"

"Of course. Having a dog as a mayor would be entertaining."

"He has been around for a long time. Do we know how old he is?"

"No. Some of the older folks claim that he's been around since they were children. Our very own local legend. The ever-mysterious Mayor Dusty Toes."

Maybe Viv was right...

"Speaking of dogs..." Luce grinned and walked over to a cabinet. "I have an idea for what we can do while we wait for the cookies."

"Luce..." Joey started, glaring at her. "What are you planning?"

Luce pulled out a small winery shirt. "We ordered more shirts for the workers, but the company messed up and sent us the wrong sizes. I thought we could still use them."

"For?"

She walked over to one of the dogs and held the shirt up next to him. "I think they would fit."

"They would look cute..."

45

"Help me get them on."

Sometimes I still feel like I'm with her. Fitting worker uniforms on dogs is something she would have done. "I hope we don't get into trouble for this," I said.

"Lorena won't mind. She might even find it amusing." Lucinda wiggled a shirt onto Bavero and grinned. "I wish we could have official guard uniforms for them. Could you imagine? Or suits and dresses! That would be even cuter."

"I don't know how much dress-up these wrinkly orange boulders will tolerate," Joey said, petting Valiant's head.

"They don't seem to mind right now. Besides, we work for the esteemed Mourlonet family. What would be a bolder statement than bragging that you have enough money to cloth your dogs in their own garb?"

"They don't like to brag."

"I know, but it would still be funny to see the look on other nobles' faces."

"I wonder if that would start a trend. If all the nobles then started dressing their pets."

"Might not be as easy to shirt a cat..."

"Some are nice, though I agree. I'd rather stick to putting clothes on our sweet dogs."

"Fanciest dogs in town right now. Too bad we don't have extra pants..."

Joey laughed. "They can't wear people pants, Luce. They wouldn't fit at all."

"Exactly why we should have specially tailored cloths for them."

"You are ridiculous."

"People make clothing for animals. I saw a parrot in a sweater in a news article once. He traveled around the world with a photographer. Needed the sweater to keep warm in the snow."

"We see cats in sweaters every time we go into your mother's room."

Luce turned toward me. "My mother has a whole shelf full of cat statues. Have you met her yet, El?"

"No."

"Why don't you head to her room and say hi? It's the one at the end of the hallway to the left. Joey and I will check on the cookies."

"Ok." *Let's see, maids' quarters are to the left, then I go down to the end. Should be this door. It's open.* I peered inside, immediately noticing the large shelf to the left filled with cat statues of all different sizes and colors. Some wore sweaters and hats. "These are adorable..."

"Aren't they?" an older woman said, walking up to me. "I'm Mary Ann. You must be Eleanora. Luce has told me about you."

"Every bit of information she knows, I'd imagine."

"She does love to talk."

"She told me you had an impressive cat statue collection I had to see."

She turned toward the shelf and grinned. "It started when Beatriz showed me some unique jade statues a while back. They were just so darn cute, I had to get them. She might have persuaded me to buy more..."

"I can see that. She can be a very persuasive woman."

"Lorena used to help me pick them out when I'd go into town, though it has been a while since she's had time to go. She's been so busy lately."

"She really doesn't get time to sit down and relax, does she?"

"Only when she goes to the music hall to practice. Helps her clear her mind. Lucinda likes to tease her about always having to be working on one skill or another to keep impressing other nobles. One big game of show-off."

"I don't think I've seen the music hall yet."

"Oh, well, it's the finest room we have. Why don't you go take a look? It's on the other side of the manor. Head toward the kitchen, go all the way down the hallway, then turn right and go to the door at the end."

"Sounds good. It was nice meeting you."

"Feel free to stop by if you need anything, dear."

Ok, down the hall, turn, go past the kitchen, turn, fancy door at the end of this wing, she should be in here... Yeah, this is one of the prettiest rooms in the manor. Lush dark red carpets, couches, and benches. They don't look all that comfortable, though I suppose they are designed to be better for posture. The walls are covered in operatic posters, bookshelves, and old family portraits, each with their own instrument. The stage is impressive. Dramatic lighting from the balcony above, well-kept vases filled with flowers lining the edge, and soft red curtains along the sides. Must be a nightmare to keep clean...

"Looking for something?" Lorena asked, walking up to me.

"Mary Ann suggested I see the music hall. She seems sweet. I got to see her impressive collection of cats."

"They are her favorite."

"Why doesn't she have a cat?"

"Lucinda's allergic. Mary Ann takes care of the strays in town. She has a little spot for them between the bank and the wood shop. She's made little homes for them, takes the old blankets and towels we don't use anymore."

"That's sweet."

"Father was a good judge of character. One look and he knew your intentions."

Oh... I'd be doomed, then. "So why here at this particular hour?"

"Practice." She sat at the grand piano. "Father was passionate about music. Mostly classical and operatic, though we would still get a chance to do something more modern and casual every now and then."

"I hadn't really heard much opera before coming here."

"You are quite casual."

"Would you prefer me be more regal?"

"I enjoy you as you are. Regality is for those who seek it."

"What if I do? I do feel a bit out of place when you have important company over."

She smiled. "Very well. Stand up straight. Try to look confident. You know who you are; show it. Hold that confidence when you walk. Every movement, every glance should be intentional and thought out. Think, then act."

"Are you truly as confident as you seem?"

"Yes, though I was raised so. You'll get there eventually. You are already staring rather confidently."

She noticed... "Hard not to."

She smiled. "You're confident with the other workers. Treat the higher class no different. Speak your mind."

"Viv was always more outspoken. She didn't really care to plan out her thoughts, just went with the moment. I'm surprised she didn't get into more trouble, to be honest."

"It isn't hard to avoid conflict if you know what to say."

"You always seem to know what to say."

"I know what people want to hear and what they should hear."

"Beautiful and smart." *I said that out loud...*

"No more than you."

What?!

She grabbed my hand and led me onto the small stage. "Try to imagine that the room is filled with high-class people. Look around the room as if they are no more important than you."

She thinks I'm beautiful...and smart... Okay, I can do this. I just need to act like she does. Think about proper and educated things and stop staring at her beautiful face.

"Eleanora."

"Hmm?"

"Focus."

"Right." *Okay, stare out at the crowd. Maybe if I picture just Viv being out there, I might feel better. She would be giving me the biggest encouraging grin right now. That always made me feel better.*

"Better confidence, but you're supposed to be impressing an entire audience. Close your eyes and focus. Sink into absolution, then open them."

I stared out toward the back. *Impress them... Impress her...*

"Better. What were you thinking of?"

"Trying to impress you..."

"You already have." She reached out her hand to help me down. "I feel like that's enough for now. Would you care to be my audience while I practice?"

"Of course."

We returned to the piano bench. Her hands glided across the keys with the same elegance she had when riding. Never a note missed, at least that I could tell. I didn't actually know what she was playing. I might have just been too lovestruck to notice.

"I assume your family all knew how to play something," I said.

51

"Father could play piano, violin, and cello. Mother tried but was rather terrible at reading music. She wasn't patient enough to learn." She took her hands off the keys and looked toward the curve in the piano. "Lucian used to sing while I played. He would sit in on my practicing when he was having a rough day. He'd wander around the piano, singing away his frustrations. Father overheard one day and insisted we perform together from then on. Lucinda's sung with me a few times since the incident, though it has felt rather lonely in here."

"I'm always willing to provide company, though I think I'll let Lucinda do the singing."

"I haven't had much time for practice lately. Business has been exhausting."

"You used to come in here more often?"

"Mother and Father used to send us here when they had difficult company over, or when they needed space." She glanced toward the bookshelves along the wall. "I've read every piece, every book. Plays from across the world, the history of instruments. Though truthfully, I just skimmed the history books. They weren't quite as entertaining to a bored child."

"Did you ever perform together as a family?"

"Occasionally. We would invite trusted friends and family over. Pride is abundant in nobility, more so in those that succeed."

"Good or bad?"

"Depends on how it is used. My father used it to build our strengths and confidence. Some have more self-centered forces behind it. It can be beneficial or corruptive."

"My father didn't say it often, just in those little moments where it really mattered. When Viv and I learned to take care of the field ourselves or when we would help our mother out when she was having a rough day. He used the good side of it."

"Would he say it now, as you are?"

"Yes, even though I keep slacking to fool around with you." I leaned against her.

"Well, we could always practice some more."

"Music or confidence?"

"Confidence is essential for music. The audience can tell when you don't have enough."

"I probably wouldn't be the best musician, then."

"Just think of me. That seems to work so far." She turned toward a hand carved clock on the wall. "Time for my phone call." She stood up and gently kissed my cheek. "You're welcome to try out any of the instruments."

Did she just—Hang on... Cazzo, she already left.

"Getting physical with our lady?" Lucinda asked, walking out from behind the stage.

"Were you spying on us?"

"I was dusting." She waved the duster at me. "Just so happened to hear you two talking." She set it down and walked up to me. "A lovestruck wine maid and the lonely regal lady. Mourlonet sapphic rose. What a story!"

"One I assume you've told everyone about by now."

"Not everyone... I don't want to spoil all the fun." She began sprinkling white sunflower petals on me. "I'll start planning your wedding."

I couldn't help but smile. *Where did she get those?* "You are ridiculous."

"I'm a sucker for a cute romance."

"We're not together."

"You should be."

"What if she's not interested?"

"Then you'll just have to settle for someone less extravagant." She winked. "I'm single."

"I thought your type was fancy, problematic men. Joey told me about your affairs with Lorena's brother."

"I could go either way. You wouldn't be the first woman."

"Oh really?"

"I might have had a little too much to drink last week and slept with Joey."

"What? Seriously?"

"Yep."

Why did that surprise me? "Our sweet little angel, Joey?"

"We both had a lot of wine that day."

"You two are complete opposites."

"Yeah, it was fun. She's really ticklish..."

"We can stop there."

She grinned. "Ok... Bet you'd be fun too."

I threw some flower petals back at her. "You are insufferable."

"I'll stop when you confess."

"I can't."

"Stop doubting yourself. She told you to be confident, didn't she?"

"She did..."

"What are you two chatting about?" Joey asked, walking in.

"Romantic gossip," I responded.

"Oh, about who exactly?"

"I was recently informed that you slept with Luce."

Her face turned red. "I...uh...we...had a lot of wine. Anthony thought the batch tasted off, so we tried it and...got a bit out of hand."

"Did Anthony get drunk, too?"

"He fell asleep in the field," Luce answered. "Was a bit too wobbly to make it all the way home."

I smiled. "We are so lucky we work for Lorena."

"Yup... So...need any tips on how to please..."

I put my hand over her mouth. "I don't need the details, and quite frankly, I don't think Joey would last through that conversation without passing out from embarrassment."

"Fair enough."

"Come on, you two," Joey started. "We need to get back to work."

Chapter 7

Oh no, Luce is grinning. What madness am I going to be dragged into today?

"You will be assisting Evangeline in the gardens today," she said. "We all take turns assisting her. Do you know sign language?"

"No."

"Then stay close and just do what she says. She can't hear but she is very good at reading lips, so watch what you say."

"Alright."

"Good luck."

She led me out to a clear glass greenhouse covered in vines. Every inch of it was perfectly clean, not a single scratch or speck of dust. A short woman stood inside, watering a small pot of orchids. She stood hunched over with long, curly dark grey hair sprawling down her back. She wore basic brown gardening clothes and tall black leather boots covered in mud.

Lucinda signed a few things to her, then turned toward me. "Have fun."

Evangeline put down the hose. "Grab that box of spray bottles and follow me."

A soft haze of mist hung in the air, covering the collection of bright flowers every size and shape imaginable. Stone pathways cut through the display, with the occasional bench in front of the more impressive plants. Evangeline handed me a sprayer and had me evenly coat the flowers. Apparently, it was her secret recipe to provide nutrients and protection. Each type of flower had its own mixture. She knew exactly what went where, and how much.

It must be a nightmare to tend to this garden when she's sick or away. Nothing here is labeled. Though to be honest she doesn't seem like the type of person to let the flu get in her way. Viv would be laughing at me right now if she could see me struggling to keep up with this old woman.

Evangeline walked into a smaller shed. "The Lobelia are wilting already..." She threw back a bunch of twigs. "How'd this get in here?" An old pumpkin rolled out. "Ah hah!" She turned around, handing me a bag of seeds. "Perfect for the new flower beds."

I could see Joey and Lucinda giggling by the back door as they watched us in the garden. Evangeline raced around, trimming this, weeding that, then turning back to water something else. I didn't really understand the method to her madness, but considering every petal was flawless I didn't see reason to question it.

Lorena eventually joined them, sipping her tea with a smile. I couldn't help but stare. She was in a simple white tank top and pants. Her bright red necklace shone in the sunlight. *Beautiful... Stop getting distracted. Where did Evangeline go? That woman walks so fast. I wish I had that much energy. Even a fraction of it would be nice. Is that her? Nope, it's a goat. Is that the same one that keeps staring at me? He probably shouldn't be here...*

"Pete!" Michella yelled. The goat darted past me. "Get back here! Eve is going to cook you if you touch any of her flowers."

I guess he gets out often.

"What is going on?" Evangeline asked, stepping out of the greenhouse.

Michella darted through a bush, barely missing him. He let out a loud bleat and continued running through the flower beds. "Don't you laugh at me, you menace!"

Viv would be able to catch him.

Evangeline reached over and grabbed Pete, holding him still. "No you don't, pesky thing." She walked him over to Michella. "Take your wild beast away from my flowers. That damn thing gets out too much."

"Doesn't help that you keep leaving the garden gate open."

"Get me my own water pump and I won't have to."

Michella smiled and turned toward me. "On garden duty today, El?"

"Yeah."

"Tired yet?"

"Very."

"I sometimes help Eve out when she's not being too bossy."

Eve waved a hand at her. "My attitude gets stuff done."

"I'm not bossy and I still get all my work done."

"Maybe you should be, it might stop that one from escaping all the time."

"He's a goat, Eve. He'll just sass me back If I do that."

"That's why I work with flowers. I don't get any complaints."

Michella hoisted Pete off the ground. "Better get him back. Good luck, El."

Guess that means I'm back to chasing Eve around. Great...she's already disappeared again.

-

I sat down in the lounge, giving into my exhaustion. "That has to be the fastest gardening lesson I've ever had. She never did tell me what we planted."

Lorena sat next to me, handing me a cup of tea. "She's a handful."

"No doubt. How long has she been deaf?"

"Since she was eight. Tried to help her father calm the cattle during a storm and got kicked in the head."

"Ouch."

"We like to tease that that's where she got her stubbornness from."

"Theres no reasoning with her, is there?"

"None whatsoever."

"At least she knows what she's doing. I only got to sit down once for lunch. Every second was heaven. Almost fell asleep on the table. If she's this energetic now, I can't imagine what she was like as a child. She must have been a handful."

"I hope it wasn't too bad. Are you enjoying working here?"

"Yes. There's always something to occupy my time. The diversity of it is nice. Were you looking for help? Rodger didn't say much before we got here."

"We weren't, though we definitely needed it."

"I'm sure the others enjoyed getting a break from garden duty."

"It was rather entertaining."

"Glad to be of service."

"Mother used to have me and Lucian help Evangeline when we were getting too energetic. It's a good way to calm children."

"Did you ever have enough energy to keep up with her?"

"Sometimes. Lucian was quicker than I was. It was more enjoyable as a child. Spending the day running around in the garden was twice as fun as sitting at a desk studying or practicing etiquette."

"I'm guessing you learned sign language pretty young?"

"Mother taught us as we grew. Lucian always wanted to impress, so he decided to learn Italian and French signing as well."

"How long did that take?"

"He knew all three forms of sign and spoke perfect French and Italian by his fourteenth birthday."

"Smart kid."

"Well, we did have the best tutors."

"Must have been easy not having to run to the school every morning."

"You'd think so, though Lucian still often showed up to lessons late."

"Even nobles have flaws?"

She smiled. "No one is excused from follies. No matter how small or how well hidden, everyone has them."

"Even you?"

"Many, according to some, though I don't like to focus on ideologies of perfection."

"Neither do I."

"Then we'll work well together." She turned toward the clock. "I have an appointment this evening. Feel free to relax for the rest of the day. Try not to let Lucinda exhaust you anymore."

"I'll try, but it won't be easy."

"Good evening, Eleanora."

"Evening, Lorena."

Chapter 8

I stepped into the kitchen, completely covered in grape juice. Josephine raised an eyebrow. "Eventful day?"

"Anthony and Gerome were having a dance battle. Gerome ended up falling out of the vat and onto me."

"Why don't you go change and take a break? We're going to be up late tonight."

"Why?"

"Lorena's been invited to a party. One of the typical posh get-togethers where people brag and complain about the lower class. We always wait for her to get back so we can hear the latest gossip."

"Cozy evening?"

"Yes, wear something comfortable."

I wonder if those parties are as fun as Viv said. She always daydreamed about them. I'm sure she would cause all sorts of mischief if she got the opportunity to go. I walked out the door and heard a stern voice echo through the hallway. *Sounds like Miss Evarchest is in the lounge. Yep, tall woman with curly light brown hair and dark blue eyes, in a red suit as always, and is holding papers in her hands. I swear she never puts them down. I've even seen her carrying some on her breaks. What are they, anyways?*

She put her papers under her arm and aggressively stirred her tea. "You need to be direct with them, Lorena. Assert the same position that your father did." She noticed me walk in. "Ah, Eleanora, how are things in the winery?"

"Good. Production is running sort of smoothly," I responded.

"As expected. We were just discussing tonight's activities."

"The rich fools party?"

"Yes. They are held fairly often at the Anfirio estate. It's a rather grand place, heavily decorated in the finest of art pieces from around the world. Only noble families are allowed to step foot in it. Dress your best and be ready to talk business. Not as fun as people think. I, for one, don't care to attend, though Lorena would prefer some company."

"Would you wish to accompany me, El?" Lorena asked.

Me? ME... "I'd love to."

"Do you have a nice dress?" Evarchest asked.

"Yes."

"Mary Ann can make sure it's proper for the party. Let Lorena do the talking, though you should still show confidence," she said, tapping me with her papers. "No nonsense."

Lorena stood up. "I'll meet you in the entry hall when you're ready."

I'm going to a fancy party with Lorena... I'm going to a fancy party with the woman I have a crush on. Viv, help me.

I walked back to the maids' quarters. Mary Ann stood by the couch, slowly folding laundry, completely unfazed by Lucinda dancing around her. "You alright, dear?" she asked.

"Lorena's taking me to the party with her."

Lucinda threw the sheet she was folding. "Really! How exciting. I can't wait for you two to dance passionately in the moonlight, surrounded by flowers."

Mary Ann smiled. "You'd better get ready, then."

"Could you help me pick out a dress?" I asked.

"Of course." She turned toward Lucinda. "Finish putting the sheets away."

"Fine, Mother..."

"Come along, El. I know you have some lovely dresses. Lorena will probably be in her new blue dress. Let's try to find something that matches." She followed me up to my room. "Is this your first regal party?"

"Yes..."

"No need to be nervous. No one will bother you as long as you stay close to Lorena. Why don't you spruce up a bit while I pick a dress?"

"It's been a while since I've worn makeup. Viv used to do it for me. She was much better at it than me. I can imagine her getting just as excited as Lucinda, prancing around the room, telling me to be confident, though I'm sure Vivienne would do whatever she could to go with so she could flirt around with the higher-class men."

"Sounds like she would fit right in. Ah, this will do fine," she said, pulling out a dark green dress. "The rose patterns on the waist of this one should match Lorena's."

"Is it important that we match?"

"No...but it would be cute. Have fun. Don't let anyone push you around."

"Thanks, Mary Ann." I stared at the dress. *Vivienne got it for me for my birthday.*

"You'll turn heads."

"I'm not sure I want to do that."

"Come on, you deserve the attention. You're gorgeous."

"Okay, okay, but you have to promise you'll stick with me for this one. I don't really want to be alone."

"I promise. I'll even help keep creeps away."

"Thanks, Viv."

"Now hurry up and get dressed before Dad changes his mind."

-

Lorena stood by the front door in a nice dark blue dress and matching eyeshadow. Her hair was held back, exposing most of her neck and shoulders.

Beautiful.

"Ready?" she asked.

Cazzo, how long have I been staring? "Yes."

"Come along." She took my hand and led me out to the carriage.

Anthony was right, this thing is very fancy. "Gloris and Vinyara?" I asked, resting my hand on one of the horses.

"You remembered," Michella said, sitting in the driver's box. "They're our biggest and strongest. Work perfectly together."

Of course the interior is just as extravagant as everything else. Black cushions, golden paint along the trim, and a soft red carpet beneath our feet. "How far away is it?" I asked, feeling the carriage roll forward.

"Not far. The estate is on the other side of town. Would be faster in the car, though Frolont hasn't driven it since the incident. Lucian was fascinated by it. Frolont had taught him how to operate it. He would take it to every event and talk about it for ages. Frolont just hasn't had the heart to drive it again."

I forgot how dark it gets in town after the sun goes down. We really need more streetlamps. The pub looks lively as ever. Even the old candle shop is full. Seems everyone's out tonight. Oh, there's the bakery. It's been a while since I've visited. I wonder how they're doing.

"You haven't been in town since you started working for me, have you?" Lorena asked.

"No."

"Did you used to visit often?"

"Viv and I did most of the errands after Dad hurt his knee. Our favorite stop was the bakery. We liked to watch the owners competing over who could make the best pastries. We'd get home late with a bag full of odd muffins.

Mother would roll her eyes, asking if we could just come home with a normal order for once, then father would come in eager to try something new."

"Sounds fun."

I stared into the bakery windows as the carriage rumbled past, watching the two bakers toss around fresh dough. "Our last visit was the day before the fair. Vivienne told them all about the event, eager to see all the interesting new things people would bring."

"Food, art, competitions, weird looking chickens, it will be exciting!" Viv said, jumping out of her chair.

Ennette smiled. "Envar refuses to go after being embarrassed by the traveling bakers son last year."

"Are you going?"

"No, sadly, I have to go to Fieldsbend for a shipment."

"Guess I'll just have to try all the pastries by myself, then."

"Just don't feed them to the animals this time."

"You won't be there to stop me."

You won't be there to stop me...

We passed by a simple dirt road with an older street marker: *Vionell rd.* I turned away from the window, looking down at the floor.

"Are you okay?"

"I used to live down there," I explained.

"Memories now scarred with sadness?"

"Vivienne tried to convince me to go with them, but I've never been a huge fan of noisy crowds."

"Neither have I."

"Last time...the fair a couple years ago, she bought some fancy green muffins. I don't remember what they were made of, some sort of tea muffin... She ended up dragging me over to the barn. Fed most of them to the pigs." My ears focused on the sound of the hooves, the noise of the carriage, echoes of screams I never heard. "Ennette told her not to do it again this year. Viv joked around, saying that no one would be there to stop her... Maybe if I had gone... I just can't get over the thought that it might...she might have... She was right there by the gate and..."

Lorena reached forward and took my hands. "Blame is dangerous, even if you mean no true malice by it. Whatever happened, happened. We can't fix that. There is no point in worrying over the dead. It's their turn to worry over us. Even if she was responsible, I'm sure she would be happy that you were spared."

"I..."

"Eleanora, I will never blame you, or your sister."

I looked up into her eyes. This look was new—softer, more concerned. I didn't want her to look away, but she eventually did. Shining gold caught my attention. We were approaching two large golden gates that guarded a massive tan and white estate covered in intricate carvings and statues.

"They own multiple beverage companies," Lorena explained. "Extremely wealthy."

"I see that."

The driveway curved around a large stone fountain. Fancy cars and carriages lined the front of the manor. Two butlers stood on either side of the door, holding lists and greeting guests with a smile. The interior was filled with paintings, statues, and various art pieces from around the world. I stopped just inside the door, admittedly a little overwhelmed. Two large blue banners stretched along the back wall. Both showed an Ibex with a sword tangled in its horns. *Anfirio* sat above it in bright white letters.

A boringly average man in a boringly average suit walked up to Lorena. "Grand and exquisite, my lady." He reached out to kiss her hand. "Would you care to accompany me?"

She glanced back at me. "We have business to attend. Perhaps later."

He nodded respectfully. "Of course."

We continued past the main ballroom, heading up the stairs to a smaller section filled with soft regal couches and large windows to the right. A number of well-dressed people stood near a round table, laughing about profits. The grandeur of the event was starting to make me feel a bit out of place.

"Brought company?" a man asked, standing by the railing. He was of average height, with short sandy-blond hair, brown eyes, and a light grey suit with a matching top hat.

I wonder why he didn't turn in his hat with his coat. That's common for upper class, right? Lucinda has been lecturing me on proper etiquette. She did give me tips for attending fancy parties a couple nights ago. I wonder if she knew...

Lorena walked up to him. "Emile, this is Eleanora."

"Lovely." He tipped his hat, staring into my eyes with a friendly grin. "Must be a lady."

I smiled. "Just a member of the staff."

"I cannot believe it. Someone as lovely as you?"

"Truly," Lorena agreed.

I could feel my cheeks redden. "Thank you."

He looked back at Lorena. "I assume you've already seen Worcard? He was waiting for you by the entrance."

"Yes. I told him we were busy."

He leaned closer to me. "He's been eyeing her for a while. Brave man."

I looked at him with a curious expression. "For desiring her?"

"Few are bold enough to try and court a Mourlonet. They are notoriously difficult about suitors."

"My family prizes loyalty and respect," Lorena said. "We have no care for those who marry and remarry out of foolish impatience or status."

"Has anyone caught your eye recently?" he asked.

"Perhaps."

He looked genuinely surprised. "Really? I assume you won't tell me. I'll just find out when the rumors make their rounds." He sipped his glass.

"What does your family do?" I asked.

"We make the finest cheeses. Nothing goes better with a good wine. Worcard is my main competitor. They use Holstein crosses. Not the best quality. Nothing beats Montbéliarde cattle. What is it you do, my dear?"

"I work in the vineyard and sometimes help the maids."

"So, you know your fair share of skills?"

"Yes, my family used to make wine."

"Really."

"Wintello Vino."

"I believe I have tried it, though it's been a while. What made you come to work for the Mourlonets?"

"The fair stampede."

"Ah, my apologies. I knew a number of good people who died that day. Awful tragedy."

Lorena glanced over his shoulder. "Would you keep each other company for a moment?"

Emile turned, looking unamused. "Of course. Good luck."

She walked over to a group of people in modern suits and dresses covered in an unreasonable amount of jewelry. Their eyes locked onto Lorena as she approached.

"Sexist fools," Emile said, taking a sip of his drink. "Mr. Smith Vintmarkel and his brother Liam are notorious for their treatment of women. They'd bed every woman they laid eyes on if they could. I do my best to avoid them."

"What are they talking about?"

"They have been trying to strike a deal with your lady ever since the incident. The two barely made it out alive but are still unbearably persistent."

Lorena walked back to us. "My apologies," she said, looking at me. "I did not wish to subject you to their antics."

"How was it?" Emile asked.

"I told them not to bother me with petty dealings."

"Were they deeply offended?"

"Yes."

"Good. That makes my day better."

Music started playing in the main hall below. People paired off and began dancing in rhythm. I glanced over to Lorena. She stared down at the crowd with little amusement. I had the idea that she wasn't the biggest fan of being here. "Do you usually dance?" I asked.

"No, though I get enough offers."

"Even some from me," Emile said. "I'm not much of a dancer myself. Much prefer hiding up here away from the crowd."

"Is there a particular way you're supposed to dance?" I asked. "They all seem to be just swaying around."

"I'll gladly show you." He took my hand, leading me away from the rail. "Alright now, ladies and lords dance with a sense of dignity and class. Nothing too wild. Now, put your hand on my shoulder, mine on your waist. We keep our other hands together. Now we just step to the side, then back, then to the other side, then forward, basically making a square."

"An elegant square?"

"Precisely. Move with an excess of confidence, like you just won the derby and had lunch with a queen and want to brag about it."

I laughed, looking back down at the crowd. Most of them held their heads high, brimming with glamor and self-worth.

"It does get boring fairly quickly," Emile said, stepping back. "Though these parties are for business more than dancing. Wish they would shake it up a bit, play some exciting music for a change."

"Then they wouldn't be able to hear their own bragging."

"Precisely." He glanced over to a clock on the wall. "Well, I've been here for a while. Talked to more than enough pompous nobles. Perhaps I'll take a stroll down to the kitchen and see what words have been floating around lately. Gossip is key. That's how you get to know the upper class without actually having to be bothered by their presence. The Anfirio estate oversees most of the noble parties, so their workers always have the best gossip around. I'm friendly enough that they don't mind me hanging around the kitchen, so I get to hear it all. You're welcome to join me, if you'd like."

"I think we'll head home," Lorena said. "I've had enough as well."

"Well, I wish you a pleasant evening."

"Same for you, Emile." She started walking toward the stairs. "Feeling alright, El?"

"Yes. I was a bit overwhelmed at first, but Emile's casual attitude made it better."

"He's a good friend of mine. Likes to differ himself from most other nobles. Keeping his hat on indoors for instance. It makes him stand out and keeps some of the more precise rule-abiders away. We've always shared similar views." She stopped at the bottom of the stairs. "Hold on. Wait for the next song to start. Everyone's attention will be in the ballroom, less likely for someone to try and stop us on the way out."

"Brilliant as always."

We watched the crowd reform as the music continued. The song grew louder, drowning out some of the chatter. Lorena continued out the door and toward the line of carriages and cars. "The ballroom will be crowded for a few more hours, then everyone will trickle back into the entry hall and balconies to finish discussions and watch drama. I do admittedly like that part, but not today."

"Ready to leave?" Michella asked, straightening her posture.

"We've had our share of excitement for the evening." Lorena opened the carriage door.

"How late do you usually stay?" I asked, sitting down.

"We used to stay for a couple hours at least. I didn't feel like staying this evening. It's my first time coming to an event like this without Mother, Father, or Lucian."

"I understand. I don't know If I could have handled hours of that."

"It was easier when I used to go with my brother, let him do all the talking and get into embarrassing situations."

"Have any particular situations you'd like to recall?" I asked, feeling the carriage lurch forward.

She stared out the window for a moment, then smiled. "One of the first parties we went to together. He was trying to impress a few of the other nobles our age. He stood back by one of the refreshment tables. Grand golden platters of the finest foods. The pair he spoke to were charming but a bit devious. He took a step back, unaware that his boot was becoming entangled in the tablecloth. The pair noticed this and decided to entice him closer. A series of crashes brought the room to a halt. Four pies had fallen, covering his expensive pants in chocolate and key lime. Lucian had to go change."

"It's definitely easier to have an energetic sibling to bring along the entertainment."

"My second favorite was his first time driving the car. He insisted on driving us to the spring celebration at the Anfirio estate. Frolont did his best to teach him, though he could have used a few more days of practice. Lucian drove well, nothing happened on the way over, though his

76

parking skills were...lacking. He ended up grabbing the wrong lever and drove the car into the wall. The look on his face was absolutely priceless."

"Complete embarrassment?"

"Like he wanted to run away to another country and never be seen again."

"Do you still have the car?"

"Yes. I can show you when we get home."

Home... That extravagant manor with all of its wild staff and overly fancy components is home. There's the gate. Joey is waiting to close it behind us. At least she has an umbrella. Still a chill night. Hope she's okay.

The carriage came to a halt. Lorena took my hand and led me to the right side of the estate to a maroon and gold car resting under a fancy brick carport.

"Father bought it from an Italian company," she said, getting into the driver's seat.

The interior was black and maroon, surprisingly comfortable, at least compared to Rodger's. "It's peaceful in here. I haven't been in many cars before. My grandfather had one we used to borrow, but it wasn't nearly as nice as this."

"It's still perfect." She ran her hand across the wheel. "Strange how the things we pour our attention into become still once we die. No matter how well it functions, how grand an idea, it closes and fades with our eyes. It's the same with status. Ever-shifting games of worthiness. A new family, the talk of the show, bold to face the eyes of nobles. Next thing, they are forgotten. One wrong move, too much money lost, and you're back to irrelevancy."

"I don't think I could ever find you irrelevant. No matter what the other nobles think. You're a bold, beautiful woman, worthy of all their respect."

She smiled softly, staring into my eyes. "I prefer to keep similar company."

She is way too good at making me blush. "You don't seem to keep much company outside of your staff."

"You are quite a collection of characters. I prefer to spend my time with those I know and trust."

"You trust me?"

"Yes. Do you trust me?"

"Entirely." Rain began pouring to the ground outside. A spark of fear shifted my eyes to the window behind her. "It sometimes still bothers me, the sound of rain...or hooves, even though I wasn't there. It makes me picture the stampede, the screaming, but when I'm with you, it's not as bad. It's just the rain. Just a horse running through a field."

She took my hand and stared out at the storm. "I used to hear it as well whenever the horses would run together in the pasture. Then I found a new distraction." She stared back into my eyes with a soft smile.

Stop thinking of kissing her. Stop thinking of kissing her.

She leaned a little closer, then paused. I got the feeling she could tell I was getting nervous. She looked down and let out a soft sigh. "We should head in before the storm worsens."

Cazzo...I missed it.

We rushed out of the car, running up to the closest door.

"How was it?" Lucinda asked, letting us in.

"Grand as ever," Lorena responded. "It's late. I'll see you two in the morning."

Lucinda waited for her to walk out. "I saw that."

"What?"

"She gave you a look. What were you two doing?"

"She wanted to show me the car."

"The car... Sure..."

I lightly shoved her shoulder. "Not what you're thinking. We just sat inside for a bit and talked."

"About what?"

"Nobility, the rain, how we're all a collection of mischievous characters."

"And what sort of mischief are you getting into? Gallivanting around with the lady, huh?"

"I just followed along."

"Like a lovestruck puppy." She took my hand. "Come on. You've got to tell us how the party went."

Josephine and Mary Ann were waiting for us in the kitchen. "So?"

"The place is beyond extravagant. I'd never seen so much food and beverages before," I said, sitting down.

"Who'd you run into?" Joey asked.

"I met Worcard and Emile. Well, we just dismissed Worcard. Emile was nice, though."

"He is way better than most of them. Has a good sense of humor and just wants to have a good time. One of the few nobles who actually get along with Lorena. Do you think he likes her?"

"He might," Lucinda responded. "Who wouldn't be enthralled by our lady? She's absolutely divine."

My mind flashed back to the party. Lorena leaning against the rail, staring down at the dance. Her dark blue dress perfectly fitting her figure. Her captivating dark eyes highlighted by perfectly placed blue eye shadow. "She's stunning."

I looked up to see Lucinda grinning at me, suddenly realizing I'd said that out loud. *I've really got to work on that.* Lucinda opened her mouth. Mary Ann placed a finger over it and glared at her.

"Were the Vintmarkels there?" Josephine asked.

"Yes," I responded. "Lorena told them to stop bothering her. She had me stay with Emile."

"Good," Mary Ann said. "They shouldn't be anywhere near women. Luckily Lorena is stern enough to deal with them. Her father used to make sure he was the one to see them. Poor girl now has to do it all herself."

"Have any of you been to one of those parties before?"

"Lorena will occasionally take one of us with her," Lucinda said. "She likes to have us keep people away. She's just not all that social, but most of them take it the wrong way and assume she didn't see them worthy to talk to them herself. They get so offended." She smiled. "I love that look on their faces."

Josephine nodded in agreement. "Completely aghast that they were told off by a maid. I'd love to do that with the Vintmarkels."

"They would probably cause a scene."

"Their funeral. People don't just cause scenes with Mourlonets. They know it won't end well for them."

Mary Ann looked toward the clock. "We should get to bed. Joey, you get to work in the gardens tomorrow."

"I'm already exhausted just thinking about it."

"Good luck," I said.

Lucinda followed me out. "You never met them, did you? Her parents."

"No."

She led me up the stairs to a larger lounge with a view of the gardens. Soft red couches and chairs sat accompanied by small bookshelves and tables. Four large portraits lined the back wall, the family crest resting at the top of each frame. The first was a man with a firm stoic appearance dressed in a fancy blue suit, his hair slicked back. His eyes matched Lorena's; deep, dark brown. Commanding and certain. Below was a bold title. *Lord Percival Mourlonet.*

Next to it was a woman in a soft, light blue dress. Her eyes were a lighter brown, matching her wavy hair. A bright blue hat rested at an angle on her head, covered in orange flowers. *Lady Lillian Mourlonet.*

The third was an energetic-looking young gentleman in a black suit. His hair was a lighter brown, tucked neatly under a top hat. His eyes were a bold medium-brown, filled with animated confidence. *Lord Lucian Mourlonet.*

The final was Lady Lorena in a dark red dress. Her hair was down, sprawling over her shoulders. A bright red jewel gleamed around her neck. *Just as beautiful.*

Lucinda stood next to me. "They were lovely people. My mother started working for them a few years after Lucian was born. I've lived in the maids' quarters since I was four. Lucian and I used to sneak down into the kitchen to play late at night. It's so much quieter without him."

"How old was he?"

"Twenty-six when he died. Three years older than Lorena. She was always the quieter one. Didn't goof off as much... I didn't believe it at first. A policeman called, told my mother what had happened."

"I didn't believe it, either," I said, following her toward the stairs. "I didn't even know until late that evening. Rodger came by to tell me. It was...weird being alone at the house."

"Well, at least you're not alone now. Goodnight, Eleanora."

"Goodnight."

Chapter 9

A perfect morning. Breakfast gossip followed by a stroll through the courtyard, trying not to get hit by whatever weeds Evangeline is throwing around. Always keeps me on my toes. Looks like Anthony is back.

He smiled and shook his head. "I can already hear him yelling at someone inside. Was he like this yesterday?"

"Yes, and the day before."

"Sorry to leave you with that. We weren't supposed to be gone for that long. The guy mixed up our order. Tried giving us a truck full of old straw. Had to lecture him on the diets of spoiled rich horses."

"Hopefully he'll lighten up now that you're back. He can go back to supervising."

Anthony opened the door. "For a professional Pinot Noir grower, he is a mess in the wine room."

"He cracked a barrel yesterday. Blamed it on me and Gerome."

"Sounds about right."

Frolont stood next to one of the crushers. "Why isn't this thing working? Incompetent workers break everything."

Gerome walked up to us and whispered, "he broke it last night trying to clean it."

Frolont turned toward us. "Anthony. Finally, a semi-competent worker. These fools know nothing of perfection." He took a swig from his bottle. "Imbéciles."

"I'll take care of it, sir," Anthony said.

"Good." Frolont walked out.

"He isn't even trying to hide it anymore."

Gerome walked up to the crusher, fiddling with the broken part. "You know he's drunk when he starts throwing French insults. I swear that's the only part of the language he knows."

"Do you know what he's saying?"

"Nope. Don't know a word of French."

"He could be saying any random shit to us." Anthony leaned closer to the machine. "What's it need?"

"A new gear."

"There's a box of them in the basement."

Luce was complaining about having to work in the basement today. I know she likes to eaves drop. I wonder... I stepped closer to the tunnel door. "Hey Lucinda, can you get it for us?"

She popped her head through the door. "Okay."

"How'd you know she was in there?" Anthony asked.

"Lucky guess."

"You know this place better than I do."

"I'm getting the hang of it."

"You went to the fancy party last night?"

"Yes."

"Go dancing with anyone? Catch any eyes?"

"Emile showed me how to dance properly, but I wasn't really looking around..."

"Are you sure?"

"I get nervous in crowds. Besides, I'm not noble. I shouldn't be looking around at events like that."

"You're cute. I'm sure you caught a few eyes."

"I didn't notice..."

Lucinda ran in carrying a small cardboard box. "She was too distracted staring at Lorena."

"Really?" Anthony asked, smirking at me.

I reached for the box. "We have work to do..."

She lifted it above her head. "Or you could go to the main lounge, maybe give Lorena some comfort before her meeting with the Botligs."

"Are you just being pushy or did she ask for me?"

"She asked with her eyes. You know, that 'oh I wish I was spending time with that beautiful new gal instead of pompous fools' look."

Anthony chuckled. "That's a very specific look." He nudged my shoulder. "Won't be able to do much until the machine is fixed. You should go have fun with your lady."

"Are you sure?"

"Of course."

Luce grabbed my hand. "Come on."

The wind is picking up. At least I don't have to deal with Frolont anymore today. I wonder if he ever gets cold. He sits on that truck with the same thin jacket every day. Guess drinking wine all day helps...

"You good?" Luce asked, opening the kitchen door.

"Just thinking."

"About?"

"Frolont has been yelling more."

"You should mention it to Lorena."

"I was going to, but I get distracted. I walk into the manor and most of my frustrations melt away. Especially when I'm with her..."

"Could you get any more lovestruck?" She twirled around me. "Eyes fancying the noble lady of the house, lost in dreams of courtship."

I blushed. "You are insufferable."

"It's cute and entertaining. I can't wait for you to confess your desires."

"I shouldn't. It isn't my place."

"It could be. She does bring you up fairly often."

"Does she?"

"Yes. She always asks about you if she hasn't seen you in a while. She gives you *the* softest eyes. She's definitely interested in you."

"You're being hopeful."

"And you're being a downer."

"Not everyone can be as confident as you. Me and Joey have to pick up the slack every now and then. Speaking of, where is Joey? I haven't seen her today."

"She went into town to get something repaired at the blacksmith's."

"Alphonse?"

"Yup."

"That's the man she likes to ramble about, I assume?"

"She goes on and on about him all the time. I can't count how many times I've heard her talk about his dreamy hair and muscular figure."

"I think I'd met him once before, though I didn't pay nearly as much attention as she did..." *Viv would ramble like that, though usually about men in general. I've probably heard her ramble about the same guy, though I don't entirely remember. She talked about men so often I never was able to keep track of all the names. Viv did seem to know everyone in town. I wonder if she ever spoke with Lucinda or Joey. She probably did. She was the social type.*

"He is pretty good-looking, though not really my type, and I have a feeling buff men aren't really your type either."

"Nope."

"Lorena's far prettier."

"You ever have any desires for her?"

"No. I always liked her brother more." She winked and pushed me into the lounge.

There she is, in her usual spot, surrounded by the dogs. Bavero's snoring is so loud... "The Botligs again?" I asked, sitting next to her.

Lorena took a sip of her tea. "Every Friday."

"Do you have to attend every meeting?"

"I don't have much of a choice. My brother was better at dealing with them."

"You can't hire someone to take care of it for you?"

"Father always insisted that we deal with our own matters, and I'm admittedly not as good at judging character as he was."

"You are only one person. You can't deal with all the company matters by yourself."

"Perhaps not. Would you be willing to accompany me? It would be nice to have someone reasonable around."

"Of course. When does it start?"

"When I walk in." She took one last sip of tea and stood. "Let's get this over with."

Miss Evarchest stood outside the room, pacing. "The Botligs are already inside."

"All of them?" Lorena asked.

"Yes. They don't seem to be in any particular mood today. Hopefully this goes quick." She opened the door.

Those three must be the Botligs. They look well dressed, absolutely beaming with arrogance.

Mr. Botlig gave me a quick glance, then returned to his papers. He was a rotund older man with a top hat covering his bald head. Next to him was an equally round woman with a pink floral dress, white gloves, and a cautious look on her face. The third was a younger man near my age who gave a slight nod and a smile as we sat down.

"Let's begin," Mr. Botlig said, standing up. "Profits are stable, just as last week. The business is thriving, though we could stretch even higher."

"We will when winter kicks in," Ms. Evarchest ensured. "As long as we don't have any more…mishaps." She glared at him with disproval.

"Do not accuse me of fault. The driver was given clear instructions. His incompetence is his own."

"You hired him."

"He was recommended by Lord Anfirio. I assumed he would be up for the task."

"You demanded he drive a carriage through a foot of snow. If you had waited for the road to clear properly, we wouldn't have had any mishaps."

I leaned closer to Lorena. "Is this how it usually goes?"

"Unfortunately. Miss Evarchest and Mr. Botlig have never gotten along. I'm not sure what started their ritual of intense arguing during meetings. Father was good at keeping them on topic, at least. Last time they rambled about types of carriage wheels for a solid half-hour."

"At least the other two seem more civilized."

"I'm sure they are accustomed to Mr. Botlig arguing through every task."

"Doesn't seem like a nice life."

"People do odd things to reach their goals. Success, power, money, fame. Some people would do anything for a name. A word given meaning through action and reputation."

"I doubt many people see their name and smile."

"They built it on business alone. Sharp words and greedy ventures. He boasts and holds the room's attention while she sits back and analyzes everyone. A well-functioning pair, at least."

"Were they arranged?"

"No. Ms. Botlig walked up to him at a ball and demanded to marry after hearing him win a debate about railway economics."

"Strong woman."

"Excessively."

"I wonder how people see my family name. We weren't nearly as well-known."

She smiled. "Yours wasn't based on power hungry desires. It was based on a family. That deserves more respect than any of the nobles who claim significance."

"Your family was both well-known and respected but still a loving home."

"One you are now a part of."

Home... My home. Here with her. I love that but hate that I had to lose everything to get here. Mom, Dad, Viv... I'm sorry. I miss you. I wish you could see this place, hear its stories, go on adventures with me, Luce, and the others. Mom and Dad could help with business matters. I'm sure Viv would love to put the Botligs in their place and get an opportunity to chat with other high-class fools. Maybe she could have found herself a good man. Maybe if I had tried keeping her home with me...

Lorena grabbed my hand and gave me a concerned look. "El?"

"I'm okay, just got lost in my thoughts again."

"Those two are done with their yelling. We can leave while they finish paperwork." Lorena stood and nodded at the Botligs. "Good day."

Ms. Botlig nodded and smiled. "Good day to you, too."

"Did anything actually get accomplished?" I asked, following Lorena out. "It seemed a bit pointless."

"The Botligs insist on frequent meetings. They want to make sure everything remains successful."

"And boring."

She smiled. "How have things been in the winery?"

"Frolont has been getting more...unfriendly."

"How so?"

"He's been yelling. More at me than the others. I thought it was because I was new, but it's gotten worse over time. Especially when Anthony isn't around."

"Why didn't you tell me?"

"I...forgot. We'd been busy."

"I'll have a word with the other workers. If he gets out of line, come straight to me, okay?"

"Okay."

Chapter 10

It's a bright, sunny morning. Only a few clouds. The forest is lively with birds, squirrels, and a pair of cackling foxes. And now Bellezza is chasing them around. I guess she found their cackling offensive. I am once again the center of entertainment. Sometimes they just need to run.

Her hooves weren't as loud, not as harsh of a reminder, but my body still tensed up. I could picture Vivienne leaning over the fence to feed the cows. Dust and broken boards. Dead bodies... I didn't think I could be so haunted by a scene I never saw.

Bellezza stopped and looked back at me, gently nudging my leg with her nose. I rested my hand on her neck and took a deep breath. "Thanks, Bell." I wasn't sure how she knew or if she really understood what was going on, but she always seemed to notice when I'd get nervous.

"They'll surprise you. They feel more deeply than some people."

"Are you okay?" Lucinda asked, catching up.

"Yeah, hopefully she got her energy out."

"Let's try to have a nice, relaxing stroll. Baketrot can lead the way. He's calm." She let go of the reigns and laid back to let him wander wherever he pleased. He wasn't really sure what to do, kept looking back at her, expecting direction. She just stared up at the falling leaves, talking about the colors. How well the reds matched the couch in the lounge, and the orange of the kitchen walls. I was too scared of Bellezza rushing off again to try it myself. I was content just listening, understanding the view through Lucinda's eyes.

"Going to lay there for the rest of the day?" I asked.

"Just until we find the perfect spot."

"Here is pretty nice," Joey started. "Beautiful view of the neighbor's fields. A nice, shaded spot by this tree, perfect for..."

Bellezza raced past, leaping over the fence. Sheep darted away from her thundering hooves. If they were too slow, she would jump over them, weaving and dancing though the herd with organized madness. I could hear Lucinda yelling for her to come back. *Not again... Damn, Viv would love riding you. You have more personality than all those nobles who flood the parties. Lillian must have been a wild individual.*

An older man with a cane slowly hobbled out of the house at the center of the field. "You again! Get away, ye circus animal."

Bellezza shook her head at him, then raced back toward the fence line.

"Are you okay?" Joey asked.

"This horse is going to be the death of me," I said, getting down. "Was weird...the old man recognized her."

Joey laid out a blanket. "Lady Lillian was a bit of a troublemaker. Wouldn't surprise me if she used to mess with his sheep for fun."

Lucinda set her picnic basket on the blanket and pulled out a sandwich. "This would be better with tea."

"It's not a great idea, riding around on a horse with a tea set full of hot water."

"Fair enough."

I hope Lorena's doing well. If only she could be here with us, sitting on the blanket in the shade of the tree. I can picture her giving one of her philosophical lectures, adding depth to the world around.

"Eleanora...? El?"

"Yeah?" I looked up at Lucinda.

"Daydreaming about Lorena again?"

"It's easy to tell," Joey started. "You always have the same smile."

Luce laid back against the grass. "The same one you get when thinking about Alphonse." She threw a white sunflower at her.

Joey threw it back. "Reminds me of how you used to look at Lucian."

"I admit my feelings unashamedly."

I laughed at that. "Do you even know what shame is, Luce?"

"No," Joey said. "We've both seen her wander around naked while she waits for laundry to be done."

Luce smiled. "It gets too hot in the summer..."

"What about the time Mary Ann caught you sneaking back in your room at three in the morning? You flat-out said that you were sleeping with Lucian, with absolutely no hesitation."

"I'm honest."

"Blatantly."

I looked back toward the manor and got a face full of flowers. *Where is she hiding all of those? She always has them ready to throw.*

"Hey, sapphic daydreamer," Lucinda said. "She'll be okay. It's just a cold. Enjoy the fresh air. We have the whole day off."

I want to, but more than anything I want to enjoy it with her.

"What do we want to do next?" Joey asked.

"We haven't left in a while. Maybe a trip into town," Luce suggested.

"Perfect. We can go visit Alphonse..."

"*You* can visit Alphonse. I don't feel like watching you stare at him while he talks about metal. Where would you like to go, El?"

"The bakery," I responded. "I know the owners. Haven't seen them in a long time."

"Then it's settled. Let's pack up and go."

"I'm not sure I like the idea of riding Bell into town. I can't even begin to imagine what all she would try to jump over..." *Oh no, Lucinda's got that grin on her face.*

"I know what we can do. You two put the horses back and I'll meet you out front."

-

Unpredictable. Absolutely, unfathomably unpredictable...and I'm doing nothing to stop it.

Luce grabbed the wheel. "Lucian showed me how it works." She turned the key and shifted the gear. The car started rolling forward.

"Are you sure about this?" Joey asked, nervously sitting in the back seat.

"Of course."

"Have you ever actually driven it before?"

"No, but it can't be that hard."

Oh no... Don't kill us. Okay, this is going well so far. She's actually driving better than my grandfather. Helps that this car is in better condition. I looked over to Luce. She smiled and waved at a few concerned people walking by. *I guess no one really trusts her behind the wheel.*

Familiarity and nostalgia wrestled in my head, reminding me how long it had been, how different things were. I'd never been in town without Vivienne before. *The roads need repaving. The butcher shop is still getting repaired. Old Dusty Toes is slowly making his way down the main road, wagging his tail at every passerby.*

"Okay, we're here," Luce said, parking the car and getting out.

Joey opened the door and smiled. "I'll go check on our latest order from Alphonse."

"Let me know if he needs any tips on how to please you."

Joey's face turned red. "Shush. Keep your mouth closed when we're out in public."

"Have fun."

I put my hand on Luce's shoulder. "You love teasing her about that."

"She's cute when she blushes."

"Going to get serious with her?"

"My heart will always belong to Lucian."

"Fair. Where do we want to start?"

"Let's see... Ooh!" She grabbed my hand. "The odds market."

Of course that would be her first pick. It's filled with all sorts of trinkets from any time, anywhere.

The owner was Beatriz Beatro, an eccentric old woman who was always covered in jewels and crystals. Her sons traveled around the world with a shipping company and would bring her crates of odd things to sell in her store. Vivienne and I helped them unpack once. It was a crate from Scandinavia, filled with jewelry, shoes, scarves, and little horse statues. Beatriz stood nearby rambling about each item. Vivienne wasn't really paying attention. She was far more interested in chatting with the younger brother. I think his name was Ron, or Rod? Something like that.

Beatriz smiled. "Eleanora and Lucinda. An odd pair."

"She works with me now," Lucinda explained.

Beatriz raised an eyebrow. "Your lady has an eye for beautiful women."

"Quite the eye." Lucinda glared at me with a playful smile. "We have the day off."

"So you decided to meander? I have a whole new collection of wares from Egypt. Golden statues, hand-carved sphynx charms, and extravagant jewelry. The Anfirio sisters have already come by to pick out the most eye-catching pieces: a tile mosaic and a collection of rare hats."

My eyes darted around, trying their best to make sense of the cluttered shelves full of bright colors and odd shapes. There were tea sets, glass statues, seashells, ornaments, weird candles, and odd-looking books just on one shelf alone. Beatriz continued on about the history of the pyramids. I couldn't recall a single moment where that woman wasn't talking. She didn't even let Lucinda get a word in.

My eyes stopped on a necklace of a black horse covered in roses. *Of course I would immediately find something that reminds me of her.*

"Whatcha got?" Lucinda asked, stepping closer. "It's beautiful."

"Reminds me of Lorena."

"You should get it for her. Shower her with gifts of affection." She gave me a tight hug.

"Shower who?" Beatriz asked, walking up.

"She's in love with Lorena."

I froze and stared at Beatriz. *Why did Luce just blare that out? Why am I surprised?*

Beatriz smiled, looking over my shoulder at the necklace. "Beautiful. Ronny brought that over from France. A small town somewhere near Champagne. I think it's perfect for your lady. What are you getting, Lucinda?"

"These glass flowers, and a couple cat statues for my mother."

"Great choice. Hope you two come by more often."

"We will, if Mother doesn't kill me for taking the car."

Beatriz laughed. "Lucinda, you wild thing. I'd better not hear about any accidents."

"You won't." Luce linked her arm with mine and led me out. "Where to next?"

I peered down the road, looking for a familiar sign. "This way."

We were hit with the enticing smell of freshly baked goods. Ennette and Envar stood behind the counter, fighting over a jar they couldn't open.

Lucinda smiled. "Snacks and entertainment. Good choice."

Ennette looked up at us, quickly letting go of the jar. Envar stumbled back onto a pile of flour bags.

"Eleanora!" Ennette ran over and hugged me. "I missed you. We were waiting for you to stop by."

"Sorry, I haven't really left the manor since I moved in."

"You live at the Mourlonet place now?"

"Yes. Lorena gave me a job after…"

Envar dusted himself off and joined in the hug. "I was wondering why you were with this troublemaker."

"Bake anything interesting lately?" I asked, stepping back.

Ennette's eyes lit up. "We got a new recipe book from Beatriz." She ran behind the counter and grabbed an old book off the shelf. "Egyptian pastries."

Envar ran into the back and returned with a large platter filled with odd deserts. "Mine are clearly better." He gestured toward the left side. "More authentic."

Ennette shoved him aside and took the plate. "It's been tricky finding new people to try our stuff. Everyone keeps asking if you'd eaten it and survived yet."

"I didn't know I was your official taste-tester."

"Well…only for the new foreign dishes. Some folks get a little hesitant with new things."

Lucinda was already chowing down on a soft cookie. "I will never fear pastries."

Envar smiled. "A woman after my own heart."

"Flattery will get you nowhere. My heart is spoken for."

"You're not married. Can I challenge him as a worthy opponent?" he teased.

"No one else may have my heart." She looked down at the pastry in her hand with a look of sadness. It was subtle, a rarity with her. I didn't think either of them noticed.

"Alright, I surrender."

Her mood shifted back into her signature grin. "What do you two think of Lorena?"

"She's cool, stops by every so often to browse... Why do I feel like you have an ulterior motive behind that question?"

"Elenora's in love with her."

They both stared at me with childish grins. "Really!"

Oh no... I glared at Luce. "Why do you do this?"

"I need all the help I can get to convince you to ask her out."

"Remind me to not take you places anymore."

"I'm the one who drove."

Envar grabbed my hand. "Vivienne would be ecstatic right now."

Ennette sat down. "Tell us everything."

-

"Have fun, Joey?" Luce asked, watching her walk up to the car.

"Tons. I got to meet his mother. She's very nice. Seems to like me."

"What about our order?"

"Alphonse should have our requested items done by the end of the week. He's waiting for a shipment to come in."

"Good. We should get back. It's getting dark."

"What did you two get up to?"

"We went to the odds market, picked out a few things, then I got to meet El's friends who run the bakery. Great people, though I'd probably get along with anyone who bakes like that."

"Was it good?"

"Too good. We have a bag of goodies back there with you if you want to try some."

"Ooh."

Some things don't change all that much. Still getting free food from the bakery, bringing home a bag of random foreign pastries, though now I have more people to share them with. Ennette and Envar now get a whole manor of people trying out their stuff instead of a small family. It should help them get more business if people hear they bake goods for the Mourlonet household.

Joey stared out the window as we drove up the driveway. "We're in trouble," she said, watching Michella walk out of the manor with an unamused expression.

Luce smiled and parked the car. "We're Lorena's favorites. What sort of trouble can we get into?"

Michella crossed her arms. "Lucinda, what were you doing?"

"Driving."

"This vehicle is to be operated by assigned staff only. Where did you even learn to operate it?"

"Lucian."

She frowned. "I knew you three were up to no good. Hurry up inside."

Luce dragged us through the door and handed the bag to Mary Ann. "Can you put these away for us?"

"What's going on?" her mother asked.

"Michella is upset because I drove the car."

"You did *what?*"

Luce pushed her through the door. "I'll explain later."

Michella walked in and glared at us. "Nothing looks broken."

"I know what I'm doing," Luce said.

"Stealing a vehicle you have no proper practice with? You could have gotten someone hurt, or damaged the car." She rubbed her eyebrows. "You and Lucian are the reason I have all these wrinkles. Unending stress."

"She was pretty good at it," I said.

Michella looked at me. "Where did you go?"

"We parked it near town center, then walked around. I was scared at first, but it really wasn't bad. She was careful."

She glared at Luce for a few moments. "I assume you're going to drive it again whether or not I tell you to stop?"

"Absolutely." Luce grinned.

"Are you confident enough to drive Lorena around?"

"Of course."

Michella sighed. "Very well. Crash it and I will personally dig your grave."

"We have the shovels for it," Luce teased, watching her walk out. "Why don't you go find your lady, El? I'm sure she'd love to see what you got her. Me and Joey can have everyone try out our baked goods."

I took a few minutes to wander the halls, soaking in the silence. I had a sneaking suspicion she would be away from her room, probably off reading somewhere by a window, maybe in the indoor garden. Just like the courtyard, everything was perfectly vibrant. Flowers of all shapes and sizes grew wildly around and in between one another. Stems twisted and tangled like a giant living bouquet. My eyes were immediately drawn to the bench in the corner. *Just where I thought.*

"Feeling better?" I asked, sitting next to her.

She looked tired. "A little."

"We had quite the day. Luce, Joey, and I went on a ride. Bellezza was her usual wild self, chasing around every other animal she saw, including the neighbor's sheep. She jumped right into the pasture and started jumping over them until the owner walked out and told us to leave. Wouldn't surprise me if that was another habit your mother taught her."

"I believe I remember the neighbor complaining about that. Mother was exceptionally mischievous."

"It wasn't the only trouble I got into today. Luce insisted on taking a trip into town... with the car..."

Lorena raised an eyebrow. "The car?"

"Lucian taught her to drive it. Michella wasn't too happy when we got back."

"I'm sure she wasn't."

"It was nice getting to walk around town. We visited the odds market and the bakery. Envar and Ennette were happy to see me again. They had Luce and I try some new recipes."

"Was it any good?"

"Most of it, though there was one bitter cookie none of us liked. We brought some back for people to try."

"Excellent."

I reached into my pocket and pulled out the necklace. "I did find something at the odds market I thought you'd like."

She smiled. "It's lovely."

"It's strange... I almost feel like I just spent the day with your family. Every time Bellezza charges without warning. Every time Lucinda actually sits still for once and reminisces about Lucian. Living in their home, hearing the stories, living in a world they influenced. I feel like I know them. Though they never spoke a word to me, I still hear their stories through the manor. Each little adjustment they did for their own comfort and style; their quirks." I looked around at the plants. "I assumed they picked what to grow here."

"They did, the irony... We grasp at the world around us, molding it to our liking. Gardens designed to defy the weaknesses of desired plants, though no matter how much we control, they will choose how to grow their leaves, how tall and large. They will defy us as we defy their fate." She placed her hand on the wall. "How these stone walls, something naturally cold and lifeless, can stop the storm and hold a comfortable warmth for those inside. Plants mere inches from the chilled air, sit behind the glass, mocking the natural order, as we mock our deaths with the changes we make. Influencing the living far after we fade."

I leaned against her, taking in the moment. Rain began tapping against the glass. I closed my eyes, relaxing. *She's always so warm...*

-

"Eleanora?"

"Hmm?" I opened my eyes. It was dark. Rain fiercely pelted the glass. Lorena had her arm around me. "It's time to get to bed." She pulled me up. "Bonne nuit, ma belle." She kissed my hand and walked out.

What's that? Not great with French...

Lucinda stood outside, dusting a windowsill. "Did she like it?"

"Yes." I yawned. "Fell asleep for a bit."

"It is getting late."

"Hey Luce, do you know what 'Bonne nuit, ma belle' means?"

She grinned. "Goodnight, beautiful."

"Oh, right…" *Wait she… Oh. Oh my…*

She grabbed my hand. "Let's get you to bed. I'll teach you how to flirt back in French tomorrow morning."

Chapter 11

I have no idea what I'm doing. I really should have paid attention to mother's lectures more. My eyes wandered over the desk. Papers were strewn over the top in no particular order. Each document was marked with sharp cursive written in bold blue ink. *All this fancy handwriting is giving me a headache.*

"What about this?" I asked, sitting on the desk, staring at a page.

Lorena tapped the pen against her lip. "I'm not sure if it's quite correct." She stood up and sat next to me.

"When does Evarchest get back?"

"Three more days."

"We can ask her then. These aren't due for another week."

"Fair enough." She set down her papers and leaned against me.

"Tired?"

"A bit. You?"

"Just a headache."

"Why don't we take a break?" She stood and took my hand, leading me out to the barn. Arkello ran up to the fence, completely covered in dirt. He rubbed his head against me. I leaned into him, scratching behind his ears.

"Thanks," I said, looking down at my shirt. *Oh well.*

Lorena led him into the barn and got out the brushes, slowly bringing the shine back to his coat. I lifted the saddle onto him, tightening it in place. His tack wasn't nearly as fancy as Bellezza's, just a simple brown leather English saddle with a soft grey wool blanket underneath. I leaned my head against him. My headache started to fade. My ears focused on the sound of her brushing out his mane, and the casual munching of hay. *Much better than shuffling paperwork.*

"Come here." Lorena's hands reached up, gently grabbing my head. Her thumbs rubbed against my cheeks. "Feeling better?"

"Mm hmm."

Her hands moved away. I opened my eyes, glaring with protest as she stepped back and swung up into the saddle. *Hey, get back here...* I hopped up behind her, listening to the sound of Arkello's hooves against the ground as we made our way out of the barn. The sun was slowly disappearing behind the manor. The fields and gardens blurred together in an array of pinks and oranges. I leaned my head against her shoulder, relaxing my arms. *Nice spot for a nap.*

Arkello slowly reached toward a vine, inching his lips closer to one of the leaves. "Arkello," Lorena said in a stern tone. "Don't touch the Noir." He pulled his head back, looking around like he had no idea what she was talking about. "Mother used to bring me up here to watch the sunset," she explained. "Her old horse's name was Valagoro. Smaller than the rest. Fierce in his movements, though still gentle with children."

"It's stunning up here."

"More so with you."

"Tu es plus jolie." *You're prettier. I hope I said that correctly...*

She smiled. "Wouldn't it be easier for you to compliment me in your own language?"

"Lucinda has been teaching me French."

"Beautiful and smart."

"I'd learn any language just to speak to you." *Definitely didn't steal that line from a foreign man who tried to flirt with Vivienne once...*

"Glad to see you more confident."

"Still trying to impress you."

"Any particular reason?"

Just in love with you, that's all... "Does there need to be?"

"No."

She always made me feel so relaxed and understood, then the voice of uncertainty would waltz into my head and remind me that my emotions were getting out of hand.

"Your confidence is fading," she said.

"How can you tell?"

"Your heartbeat is speeding up."

"Might have something to do with me trying to flirt with a proper lady."

"Don't worry about the words, just relax and say what comes to mind."

I haven't built up that much confidence yet. I could see the workers down the field, packing up their gear. Evangeline stood at the bottom of the hill, watering plants. *Don't get distracted. Come on, El, think of something to say.*

Lorena broke the silence. "You are more fun to flirt with than most."

"I'm sure you've heard all the compliments."

"The same words in different tones, all holding the same hollow meaning. Nothing more than a desperate grasp to hold onto their titles by reaching for mine. You don't have the same illusion to your words."

"I genuinely do like spending time with you."

"I feel the same."

I felt like I should say something, any form of clarification. It shouldn't have ended there, but I was running out of rehearsed phrases and basic compliments. I didn't just want to say everything she'd already heard. *What would Viv say? I'm thinking too much... Great, my headache is coming back.*

We made our way around the vineyard, listening to the evening birds and squirrels running around the nearby trees. *So much easier to ride when the horse pays attention to us and not every woodland creature around. He's just as energetic but far more controlled...just like Lorena.*

Michella met us back at the barn. "Enjoy your ride?"

"Yeah," I said, helping Lorena down.

She glared at us with an eyebrow raised. *What? Oh, my arm is still around Lorena.* I took a step back and sat on the fence, watching them disappear into the barn. *The stars aren't out yet. I wish they were. It would be a nice distraction from my emotions. Should I ask her about it? Casually bring it up? No... I should check on the workers, see if they need any help finishing for the day. There's Anthony and Gerome. Looks like they just got done cleaning.*

"How'd the day go?" I asked.

Anthony smiled. "Not too bad. Bet you had tons of fun with your paperwork."

"We're getting the hang of it."

Gerome looked me over. "Looks more like you were lollygagging around." He grabbed a horse hair from my jacket. "What sort of 'business' is this?"

I looked down at my dirt-covered shirt. "We were in the study all day. Staring at paperwork is headache-inducing, so we decided to go for a ride."

Anthony put a hand on Gerome's shoulder. "What are you complaining about? You always look like you just lost a battle with a tornado."

"You're not much of a looker yourself, yah goddamn twig," Gerome responded.

I shook my head and smiled. "Frolont leave already?"

112

"Yeah," Anthony answered. "We'd better get home as well. My wife will be furious if I miss the carriage again."

Gerome opened the door. "It is rather amusing watching you run home."

The winery went quiet. Most of the lights were off. I leaned against the wall, feeling the cool stone against my back.

"Worn out?"

"Yup."

"Me too."

Viv's shoulder brushed against mine. A cool breeze ran past.

We used to stand against the back of the barn after a long day, listen to the sounds of the forest, feel the wind or rain until Mother would call us in for dinner. This time, there was no wind, and I was alone. I opened my eyes, staring at the shadows of bottles and machines. I couldn't quite pinpoint the feeling. Memories grasping at me through the stone, while shadows made a familiar space seem odd, all on top of my swirling emotions. It was easier when I didn't have time to think, when I was occupied with a task, figuring out a problem, or getting dragged on another adventure. My mind never knew what to do when I had a quiet moment to process my thoughts. It just ended up giving me another headache.

"Hiding in your thoughts?" Luce asked, walking out of the tunnel door.

"Headache."

"Too much paperwork?"

"And overthinking."

"I saw you went on a ride with Lorena. Ask her out yet?"

"No..."

"You should have done it. That was the perfect opportunity. Did you at least use what I taught you?"

"Yes. It made her smile."

"Perfect. You just needed to take one step closer. You're both physically comfortable with each other, and she has been flirting back."

"But she's trying to help me with my confidence. She might not mean anything by it."

"Noooooo." She placed a finger over my mouth. "No denial or pessimism. I refuse to allow it."

"But Luce..."

"No. You're thinking about it too much. You make each other happy. She'd much rather spend her free time with you than being alone."

"She doesn't exactly have many options for company."

She rolled her eyes. "You're such a downer today."

"All that paperwork gave me a headache."

"Pain is clouding your judgement."

"It went away for a while when we went out for a ride."

"Too distracted by the pretty lady?" Luce grinned. "You could always spend the night with her, you know, to relieve your headache."

"I'm not as bold as you."

"You don't have to be. She likes you for you. Just talk to her about it."

"I'm surprised you haven't done that for me."

"How do you know I haven't?"

I don't...

"We should get back to the manor. Have some dinner, then sleep away that headache, and I'll teach you some more French flirting tomorrow."

Chapter 12

I didn't even acknowledge the yelling. It had become a regular part of my mornings. Anthony met me by the door, telling another hilarious story about the worker's house. Nonstop mischief mostly brought on by foolish dares and challenges. They thought they were being sneaky, though Lorena had informed me she knew of their antics. Apparently, Evangeline liked to take long evening walks, occasionally getting a glimpse of the mischief. Evangeline told Lorena everything—she meant to clarify, EVERYTHING.

Anthony opened a new crate filled with empty bottles. "Looks good."

"How many?"

"Three crates of Noir, three of Blanc, two Rose, and one Sanguine. The Rose will need to be bottled first."

I picked up one of the clear, light pink bottles. The glass was the exact same color as the Rose. "Where do we get our bottles from?"

"Ganterco Vintage. They specialize in beverage bottles. Everything is specialty-made for our products." He picked up a red Sanguine bottle. "Unique color and shape. Makes our wines even more expensive."

"Got any wild bottling stories?"

"Had a man try to drink an empty bottle once. He was so embarrassed."

"A sober man?"

"Yep. We set the corks on top when we unpack them, get them ready for bottling. He walked in, argued with Frolont on quality, grabbed a bottle and tried to take a swig. Even Frolont laughed at that."

"Anyone I know?"

"Bartren."

"Of course. That man loves his wine."

"I should help Gerome finish unloading, make sure nothing arrived broken."

I opened the second crate. Inside was a collection of clear bottles in perfect condition. *Mourlonet Blanc. The third crate should be filled with maroon Mourlonet Noir bottles... More yelling. Something about barrel positions and the temperature of the walls. Wonder how long that's going to last.*

A loud crash made me whip around. Frolont had stumbled through the doorway, falling into the crate of Rose bottles.

"What the hell is this doing here!" he yelled.

"We just got a new shipment."

His eyes were red. His hand firmly grasped around a half-empty bottle of Noir. "I can't leave you alone for a moment without you ruining everything."

"I'm not drunkenly breaking things," I muttered.

His words started to slur. "Your foolish behavior is intolerable." He threw his bottle onto the floor. "I will not have anything ruined further." He grabbed another bottle, swinging it around as he spoke. "Tu es con comme une valise sans poignée." He threw his hands into the air, knocking me to the floor.

Anthony rushed in and pushed him back. "Drunken hypocrite."

"Incompétent! Imbécile!"

"Frolont." The room went dead silent. Lorena stood in the doorway. "What is going on?"

He turned toward her, visibly trying not to sway on his feet. "Don't worry yourself about these amateurs..."

"Quiet."

His eyes widened. "Lady..."

"I've heard rumors of your mistreatment. It will not be tolerated."

"They messed up..."

"You messed up." They stared at each other for an unnervingly silent moment. "You're dismissed."

"I am the head of production..."

She calmed her voice. "Get out."

He grabbed his hat and fumbled out the door.

Lorena helped me up. "There's broken glass stuck in your hand. Let's get you back to the manor. Anthony, make sure Frolont doesn't do any more damage as he leaves."

"Yes, ma'am."

We made our way through the garden, listening to Evangeline mutter about me bleeding all over her flowers. "Would be better if she bled on the red roses" was not a phrase I was expecting to hear in my lifetime, though from her, not exactly a shock.

"What happened?" Luce asked, watching us walk in.

"Frolont lashed out drunk," Lorena responded. "Get Mary Ann and a medicine kit." She held tight onto my wrist, carefully looking over my hand. "Keep it still."

"I'll try."

"Are you hurt anywhere else?"

"No."

Bavero sat in front of me and rested his head on my lap. *That cute face could distract anyone from pain.*

Lorena put her arm around me. "Breath slow, it will help you calm down."

Mary Ann sat in front of me. "Look away, El."

"Look at my pretty face," Lucinda said, sitting next to me.

Pain shot down my wrist. My hand jerked away from Mary Ann. She tightened her grip. "It's out." She pressed a rag to my palm. "Eleanora, I need you to calm down, your hand is shaking too much for me to stich it up."

I took a deep breath. "Okay."

Lucinda winked at me, then gently put a hand on my shoulder, slowly pushing me against Lorena. *You are going to be the death of me,* I thought, glaring back at her.

119

Mary Ann wrapped my hand. "I hope you fired that fool."

"I did," Lorena said.

"The man was intolerable. I can't believe you kept him around this long."

"It's not easy to find people who can tame Pinot Noir."

"Shouldn't be worth the abuse."

"He used to be better, before the fair."

The room fell quiet. Everyone's eyes shifted to their own corner of the room. *I wonder how many others in town feel this way. So many were lost that day. I guess Frolont couldn't handle it. He doesn't have anyone to go home to. These people were his family.*

"How long had he been working here?" I asked.

"Almost twenty years," Lorena answered. "He was highly recommended. Didn't used to drink." She sighed and set our hands in her lap. "It isn't our problem anymore. I should have done something sooner, before it escalated."

"No one expected him to do that. I always thought he was all bark."

"I don't like seeing you hurt."

"I'll be okay. I have to take it easy, so I'll just have to keep you company for a few days."

"Have anything in mind?"

"Anything but paperwork."

She smiled. "I won't make you do paperwork. How about you play my audience for the next few days? I have to catch up on piano practice."

"Sounds perfect."

Anthony walked in. "Frolont is gone. Didn't put up a fuss or break anything else while I escorted him off the property. Gerome is already planning a celebration. We're all glad he's gone, though I am curious, who's supposed to be in charge now?"

"You and Eleanora."

"Really?"

"I trust you."

Anthony looked at me. "Well, let's not disappoint. I'll be able to handle things on my own while you rest. Don't want you making that hand worse."

"I can still—"

Mary Ann gave me a stern look. "No work for you for a few days. You need to let yourself heal. I don't want you losing that hand to infection."

"Okay."

"I'll go inform Miss Evarchest about the change."

Luce got up and grabbed Anthony's arm. "We'll go clean up the mess in the winery." She gave me a wink and rushed out.

Lorena raised an eyebrow. "They seem to really want us alone."

"Luce is always being suspicious..." *Too suspicious...*

"Why don't you lie down for a bit? I can turn on the radio; help you get your mind off it."

"Sounds good."

"Music or news?"

"News."

"Lean back and get comfortable."

"Are you going to get comfortable with me?"

"Alright, come here." She wrapped her arms around me and pulled me to lean on her.

Warm...soft... Couldn't think of a more perfect situation for a nap. I closed my eyes and listened to the ramblings of the reporter. *Railway constructions... New bread recipes... Something about cars...*

My hand hurts. Why does my hand hurt? The fence... Viv and I jumped the fence. That's probably it. Part of the fence broke when I climbed over. She wanted to show me something... What was it?

"Eleanora, Vivienne, what are you doing?"

"I wanted to show El the new puppies."

Right, Billy's dog had puppies. Dad never liked us visiting his place because of the mud.

"You girls get back home. There's supposed to be a rainstorm tonight."

"Okay, dad."

Right...the storm. We almost got caught out there. I wasn't scared of the rain then. Why am I scared now? The fair... The fair... No... Viv...

"Eleanora? Wake up, dear."

That's...that's not Viv.

"El."

"Lorena?"

"Were you dreaming?"

"Yeah, about my family. I hurt my hand a few years ago climbing over a fence. Viv and I almost got caught in a storm."

"Was it a bad dream? You looked uncomfortable."

"I...started thinking about the fair again."

"I understand. My dreams are often interrupted by it, too." She pulled me up off the couch. "Why don't we think of something happier for a while? The boys have a surprise for us."

Right, Frolont is gone. Gerome wanted to celebrate. I wonder what I'm about to walk into. Anthony and Gerome aren't the wildest, so it shouldn't be too crazy. Not like I wouldn't follow Lorena anywhere. It's chilly outside...and now there's leaves in my hair. Evangeline must be nearby. I'm too tired to mind.

Lorena smiled and pulled the leaves from my hair. "Perhaps we should keep umbrellas on hand when traversing through the garden."

"Great idea."

Gerome dramatically opened the winery door. "Welcome to our glorious celebration. Joey was kind enough to bring snacks, Luce baked cookies, and I've prepared some glasses of our unquestionably pristine bottles of Rose." He handed us each a glass.

Josephine gave me a hug. "Are you feeling okay? Chef made some type of Italian soup. It's supposed to help you heal faster."

"Thanks, Joey. Is he not here?"

"He already left for the day."

"I still haven't met him."

"Really? That's odd."

Pete bolted through the door, knocking Gerome off his feet.

"Get back here!" Michella ran after him. "You keep doing this and I'll have you roasted for the holidays." Pete let out a bleat and kicked an empty barrel into her path. "Hey, don't you sass me. Get over here before you break something." He grabbed a bunch of grapes and ran out the door. "Thief!"

I smiled and leaned against the wall. *This is home.*

Chapter 13

"Following me around again, Luce?"

"I need to make sure you're not doing anything you shouldn't while you're healing. Besides, it gives me a chance to give you more romantic advice. You and Lorena have been spending a lot of time alone in the theatre."

"Alone? Don't think I haven't noticed you sneaking around upstairs."

"I was dusting."

"Sure you were."

"I was! You know how finicky my mother is about dust."

"That's why you've been dusting the same room, at the exact same time every day, for the last three days?"

"Yes... You never know when a musical professional is going to want to come over and see our glorious theatre. We have to keep it in perfect condition."

"How much should I bet that I'll see you in there again today?"

"You won't see me."

"Sounds like a challenge."

"Fine, if you see me, I'll make you a batch of your favorite cookies. If you don't, you have to make me a batch of mine."

"Deal."

Luce opened the door to the theatre and grinned. "Have fun."

Lorena sat at the piano, staring at a piece of music. "Sorry I wasn't at dinner tonight. I had to make several phone calls."

"All business related?"

"Unfortunately."

"What's this piece called?"

"'The Eyes of Miss Everfollow.' It's a softer piece."

I sat next to her as she began to practice. She rarely looked down. Her eyes scanned the pages while her hands hovered over the keys, tapping them softly, barely making any sound as she figured out the piece. It sounded like the echoes of a melody playing at a distance. I liked to close my eyes and imagine different scenarios for each song. I could picture myself standing in the woods, listening to a far away, soothing song. It grew more and more lively as I walked toward it, guiding my imagination through the notes and keys until I would open my eyes and find myself sitting next to her. I would always watch her play one final time as she mastered the piece.

Wait, are those...flower petals? I looked up to see Luce's hand dropping petals from the second-floor balcony. *Lucinda, you chaotic fairytale genius.* Lorena smiled and continued her melody. I leaned against her, watching the soft white petals sway and twirl to the floor, dancing with the music. *You would not believe what's happening to me right now, Viv. I feel like I'm in one of those romance stories Gran used to try and read to us.*

The song ended. Lorena looked at me, let out a soft chuckle, and began gently pulling petals out of my hair. "The sweetest flower."

I can't handle her compliments sometimes. Cazzo, I'm blushing again. "They go really nicely with your dress."

"Luce suggested I wear something floral today."

"I wonder why..."

"Luce?" Mary Ann started, walking up to the edge of the balcony. "Why are you doing that? The petals are going to get stuck in the piano."

"Mom, you're breaking the moment. You know every stage has to have some drama, extra finesse. It would be a crime not to drop petals on them during a song like that."

"You'd better make sure all of them get taken out of that piano."

"Of course, Mom."

"Maybe you should use full flowers next time," I suggested.

"The sunflowers are way too big," Luce responded. "They would have plopped to the ground. I wanted them to softly float."

"You can always ask Evangeline what flowers would be best for that."

"She might get confused why I'm asking her what flowers will float nicely that are big enough not to get stuck under the piano strings."

"It's you, she won't even blink at a question like that."

"Fair point."

Lorena stood. "I'm done practicing for the evening if you want to get started cleaning this up, Luce."

"Okay."

"Use the stairs. Don't try climbing down again."

"Fine."

Lorena let out a sigh. "It's getting late. Shall I walk you to your room, El?"

"I'd never say no to that. Good luck with cleaning, Luce." I followed Lorena out the door. "I always thought life in a manor would be magical."

"It would seem Luce's life purpose is to make it as fantastical as possible."

"Has she ever done that before?"

"No. It was a surprise, to be honest."

"I found it hard not to laugh when Mary Ann caught her doing it. She knew it would be a pain to clean up."

"Luckily Luce has the patience for it."

"Mary Ann's probably making her dust the piano while she's at it."

"She has been intent on making the music hall as spotless as possible the last few days."

"You noticed her sneaking around too?"

"We were raised together. She can't hide from me." Lorena opened my door. "Will you need any help getting situated? I know Lucinda has been helping you. She's going to be busy for a while."

"I'll be okay. I'm starting to be able to use my hand again. I should get back to work in the winery tomorrow. I'm sure Anthony can use an extra hand and a half." *Oh shoot... That was a missed opportunity to have her stay longer.* I could practically see Vivienne and Lucinda simultaneously facepalming at me.

She reached for my hand. "Has Mary Ann taken a look at it today?"

"No."

She slowly unwrapped it. "Move your fingers."

Gladly. Cazzo, don't think like that, El...

She smiled and chuckled a little. "Getting distracted again?"

"How can you tell?"

"Your expression shifts when you're trying to get out of whatever thoughts you're having."

"I didn't realize."

"What were you thinking about?"

Nothing... "I uh... It didn't hurt that time."

"You were too distracted. Move them again."

Focus, El. Get your mind out of the bedroom. "It still hurts a bit, but I think I can start doing some of the easier tasks."

"Then you'd better get some rest." She took a step back. The soft glow of the sunset covered her face in warm colors. "Goodnight, El."

I'd rather you stay... "Night, Lorena."

Chapter 14

"You alright?" Anthony asked with a smile.

"As alright as I can be after two hours of following the inspector around, trying not to get in anyone's way. She stared at every inch of the building with wide, calculating eyes, adjusting her large circular glasses every few seconds which bothered me for whatever reason. She didn't say much, just stared at something, scribbled in her notebook, gave an unamused 'Hmm,' and moved on."

"That's Donna. She comes in every month or so, unless something new happens and she needs to come sooner. She seems critical, but we always get a perfect score."

"Even when Frolont used to be here?"

"He always took inspection days off. I'm sure she would have chewed him out for drinking on the job."

"That would have been fun to watch. How are things going out here?"

"Good so far."

I placed my hand onto the old truck. "Why is this here anyways? I've never seen it move."

"Thieves drove it here one night a while back. It got stuck in the mud. They tried to run but didn't get very far. Valiant is crazy fast for her size. Spoiled dog."

Gerome took my hand and smiled. "My lady." He gestured for me to climb on. "You have earned it."

I stepped up, looking out over the field. *The truck is just far enough up the hill to see over the courtyard bushes and the taller plants by the barn. No wonder Frolont got away with so much slacking... He could easily see if Lorena was headed this way...* "Pretty good view."

"For us as well," Gerome chuckled.

"Damn right," Anthony agreed, sitting next to me.

Gerome threw grapes at him. "You aren't as pretty," he laughed.

"Hey!" Anthony threw them back. "Five days in and you're already trying to overthrow me."

"You're working with a woman now. You know you aren't going to be able to make any decisions."

"That only applies to being married."

"Fair point. So, what's the plan then?"

"We've been running smoothly so far. El and I can take turns supervising the winery and the fields, so no one is left in the cold for days in a row."

"Sounds good."

"Any issues so far this morning?"

"Nope. Got a few new winter workers, they're doing well. Those three over by that shovel no one ever uses."

"What are their names?" I asked.

Gerome smiled. "Phil."

"And?"

"Phil."

"And?"

"Phil."

"What?"

"Phil the first, second, and third. Don't try figuring out which is which. It's impossible."

"What do you mean?"

"They look exactly the same, even though they are from three different generations. It's nuts."

He's right. They look identical. Same hair, same face, same basic-colored clothes and everything. That's bizarre. "How are they doing so far?"

"Excellent. They know their way around the vines. Seem to be getting along with everyone. I'm telling you everything is smooth; buttery smooth. So incredibly smooth that work has actually been enjoyable."

"Is the winery doing just as good?"

Gerome led us to the building. "Having the Phils has made it easier to keep this maintained. Dottie and I have been working on getting the machinery back to perfect order now that Frolont isn't here to break it. Barrels are at the perfect temperature and the bottles have been dusted. Dottie made some new shelves in the back so we can store more bottles. We're probably the most efficient company right now."

"Aw, I missed seeing Dottie?"

"You were too busy with Lorena. She did say to give you a hug for her." Gerome put his arms around me and squeezed tight.

"Harder," Anthony laughed.

"I'm trying," Gerome said, squeezing me tighter.

"No one gives hugs like Dottie."

"No one." He let go and stepped back. "Strongest woman I know. Almost felt like I should have been the one wearing the white dress at our wedding."

"She's what, six feet tall? Almost a whole foot taller than you, old man."

"Make fun of me all you want, Anthony. I'm the one who got to marry her."

A loud clang echoed through the room. "What was that?"

Pete burst through the door. Gerome jumped up and started running.

"Shit." Anthony jumped onto a stack of barrels, barely escaping the commotion.

"How'd he get in?" I asked. *My first day back and all hell is breaking loose. Of course.*

"I don't know, but we'd better get him out before he damages our stock." Anthony jumped off the stack, running toward Pete.

"Keep him away from the vats." Gerome chuckled. "We don't want him getting drunk, he's already a menace sober."

"I've got it!" Michella said, charging in on Baketrot. She carefully maneuvered around the room, twisting a lasso in the air. Pete darted around stacks of barrels, trying to avoid her.

134

Gerome started laughing, blurting out Italian encouragements like he was at a show.

"Back to the barn, Pete," Michella said, lassoing the goat, and hoisting him up.

"Glad that didn't happen while Donna was here," I said. "We'd better check for damage." *Someone must have left a door open. Unless Pete figured out how to open them... He might have. He is crazy smart for a goat.*

"Where's that laughing coming from?" Anthony asked.

"Laughing? Oh... Luce must be in the tunnel again. Lucinda, are you spying on us?"

She opened the door. "You would be too if you were bored out of your mind. Josephine and Mary Ann got done with chores early this morning, so they told me to take the rest of the day off. Glad they did, that was crazy!"

"Are you going to be useful and help us clean up at least?"

"Fine." She grabbed a broom and started sweeping up the hoof tracks.

Of course Pete had to interrupt our moment of peace. Always something exciting going on. At least he didn't break anything... Cazzo, never mind. One of the vats is overflowing. Looks like a barrel of Sanguine got knocked into it.

"Anthony, we have a problem."

"That's unfortunate," he said. The two liquids were swirling together, fading into a light pinkish-red. "We were re-barreling and testing a few containers of Rose before the excitement."

Lucinda grabbed a glass and scooped up some of the liquid. "Probably still tastes good." She took a sip and put on an overly critical face. "Actually, pretty amazing."

"How much Sanguine per Rose ratio was it?" I asked.

"Fifty-fifty," Anthony answered, looking closer at the barrel. "Looks like they were roughly the same date as well."

"We should see what Lorena thinks."

"Lucinda, if you would fetch our lady. I'll get it fully mixed and re-barreled."

"You two are so demanding today," she said, disappearing back into the tunnel.

Anthony turned back toward the vat. "Glad Frolont is gone. He'd have a heart attack if he saw this."

"He'd probably threaten to cook Pete for dinner."

"Goat cooked in vintage wine."

"Pete would still make a better boss."

He chuckled. "Absolutely."

"Here they are," Lucinda said.

"That was fast."

"They were in the basement talking about old furniture."

One hilarious recap of our morning invasion which had Evarchest chuckling behind her handful of papers, then I was handing her and Lorena a glass, studying

Lorena's expression with hopelessly lovestruck eyes—at least, that's what Anthony said later...

Evarchest took a sip. "Intricate, floral, though not too strong. It's rather splendid. Are we producing it?"

"Yes," Lorena answered.

"Fantastic. This will quell the Botligs complaining about profits." She analyzed the glass in her hand. "We should throw an occasion to celebrate. Show off our new product. Do we have enough?"

"Two barrels," I said. "We could replicate it further."

Lorena picked up a clipboard and followed us to the stacks of barrels. "Pull two barrels of each from the June tenth batch."

I grabbed an empty Sanguine bottle. "We're going to need new bottles for this."

"I'll put in a new request. What should we call this?"

"Sanguine Rose, Sanrose, Rosan?"

"Mourlonet Rosan."

"Perfect," Miss Evarchest said. "I'll start the preparations for the event."

Lorena gently grabbed my hand. "How is it feeling?"

"Still hurts. I forget not to try and grab things with it sometimes."

"Are things going well in the winery, aside from today's adventure?"

"Much better without the yelling. Anthony and I decided Pete would be a better boss than Frolont."

She smiled. "Yes, but he would just eat all of the vines."

"Didn't think about that. Do you have business today, or would you care to observe the new wine?"

"You are far more interesting to look at than paperwork."

"And you are far more intriguing than the wine."

"Okay you two," Anthony said, standing in the doorway. "Less staring at each other and more staring at bottles. We need to get ready for Evarchest's party. You know how quick she gets them organized."

We followed him into the other room. Gerome jumped out of his chair and hid behind a barrel.

"Relax," Anthony said. "People, not goats."

Gerome sat back down. "I'm fine."

"You really that scared of a little goat?"

"He was coming right for me! Didn't seem to care about anyone else. He took one look at me with those copper eyes..."

"I'm telling your wife."

Gerome shoved him playfully. "I'm not scared."

"You can't lie to me. I've known you for twenty years." He nudged his shoulder. "Dottie is going to love this."

"You gossip so much with my wife I'm surprised she doesn't just marry you instead."

"I'm more worried about our wives realizing they're too good for us and marrying each other."

"Don't give them that idea."

Anthony laughed. "Then we marry each other to get even."

"Right then, I want a big fancy wedding in town."

Anthony threw up his arms. "Of course, you'd be a handful of a wife."

"I would." He turned on the radio. "I get to decide the music if we're married."

"Fine, but I get to lead." He grabbed Gerome's hand and started dancing.

Lorena smiled and grabbed a clipboard. "I've missed working in here."

"You're welcome anytime," I said. "Rather you than that old grump we used to have."

"He was far kinder when I was a child. He taught Lucian and I how to work some of the machines."

"Hard for me to imagine him being nice."

"He never had children of his own. Seemed to enjoy having us around."

"Maybe he's still good with kids. I've only seen him interact with adults."

"Maybe. I do hope he gets better."

"At least the rest of us are alright... I spoke too soon. Now Anthony and Gerome are fighting over who is the better dancer. And they were bragging about how smooth things were going earlier. This day has gotten wild."

"At least they're only playfully fighting."

"Now they're wrestling and getting grapes on everything... Yup, time to go."

"Lunch break?"

"Sounds perfect."

Chapter 15

"We should make Anthony our morning tea maid," Lucinda said.

Joey grinned and grabbed her hand. "Put him in one of our dresses. I'm sure we have one that fits him."

"I might be able to persuade him."

Lorena smiled and sipped her drink. "Honestly...I don't think he would oppose the idea."

"I'm sure it wouldn't be the wildest thing he's done, especially with all of Lady Lillian's tricks."

"I had a dream about her last night," Joey said. "She was standing here in the main lounge, looking out the window at a bunch of fish swimming by. We were all going about our regular days. Evangeline was happily swimming around the garden with a watering can."

"Would make wine making far more difficult," Lucinda added.

"The fish would steal all the grapes."

"Do you think we could train them to do the chores for us?"

"Your mother wouldn't let us. Speaking of, what's the schedule for today?"

Lorena looked at me. "Emile has given us an invitation to visit his estate, if you are interested."

"Yes."

"I'll drive," Lucinda offered.

Mary Ann set down her tea. "Then Joey and I will help Evangeline prepare the gardens for winter."

Joey leaned back against the couch with a defeated expression. "At least I won't have to swim. Should I have the cook make us all dinner, or will you be out by then?"

"We should be back for dinner," Lorena responded.

"Very well. Have fun."

-

The car rolled down the road at a leisurely pace. Part of me expected her to hit the gas and blast through town. All the onlookers seemed to be thinking the same thing as they watched her slowly drive by, eyes glued to our car, waiting for something to go wrong.

"Stop by the post first," Lorena said. "I have papers to drop off."

"Is that Worcard out front?" I asked, peering out the window.

"Seems to be," Lucinda said, parking out front.

Lorena opened the door. "I'll only be out for a moment." She walked up to him and smiled. "Good morning, Worcard."

He politely nodded his head. "Lovely as ever, Lorena."

141

"What brings you here?"

"I have my eye on a plot of land. We need more room to expand our herd. I'm supposed to meet with the owner, but my car seems to be having trouble. What brings you to the post today?"

She lifted the letter in her hand. "Banking business."

"Ah, papers and numbers. Not my favorite." He looked at his watch. "Seems I'm going to miss my meeting."

"Where do you need to be?" Lorena asked.

"The train station. He's too busy to travel at the moment, so I agreed to meet him at his estate in Vinehollow."

"We can give you a ride."

"I would be grateful."

Lucinda looked at me and whispered, "Bet he'll be talking the whole way. Probably try to convince Lorena to cut her deal with Emile and work with him instead."

"I guess we have to be polite and quiet."

"Just until he leaves."

Worcard opened the car door and gestured for Lorena to get in. "My lady."

"Thank you." She sat down.

"Wine and cheese, nothing is more fitting a pair," he said, climbing in. "Our company is still looking for a business partner to expand our sales."

"Sales do profit from joint efforts," Lorena said. "More variety in the people promoting a product makes it more interesting to a wider audience."

"Exactly. I've been looking into creating a contract with a local winery. Of course, they will have to be of the highest quality. Yours is quite excellent."

"Thank you, though I do already have a contract with Emile that is good for another five years."

"He is an excellent businessman. Always knows what moves to make for the betterment of his company. I'm glad you have a good deal."

Luce was right, of course. At least he is being polite about it. Still looks completely full of himself.

"How has your mother been?" Lorena asked.

"Fit as ever. She's hoping I'll marry soon," he responded. "Someone proper. You've managed to catch her attention, Lorena. No nonsense, no petty squabble, respectable, and lovely as ever." He smiled.

Lorena stared forward with a calm expression. "She is a strong woman. I'd imagine going against her wishes is out of the question."

"Firmly. Once she has a plan, she will put her full force into seeing it through."

A loud train whistle grabbed my attention. I'd only been to the station a few times before to pick up Father from business trips. Grandfather would drive his dusty old truck. Vivienne and I would talk in the back seat, waiting for the train, wondering where our father had been and what he was going to bring back. I could still smell the dirt and grape leaves that covered the floor.

Worcard opened the door, pulling me out of my daydream. "I'd love to continue our conversation when I'm finished. Perhaps you would accompany me to dinner tomorrow night? I've heard the local cuisine is spectacular."

Is he...?

"Unfortunately, I will be busy at the manor preparing for our event," Lorena responded with a calm smile. "You are welcome to stop by for tea if you'd like."

"Gladly. Thank you for your assistance." He nodded, stepped out, and closed the door.

Why do I feel nervous all of a sudden? She hasn't shown serious interest in him, though she isn't exactly the easiest person to read. Of course people will show interest in her, she is stunning and well-respected. Lucinda's been far too encouraging of my feelings...

We drove up to a smaller estate made of smooth beige stone, surrounded by bright green fields speckled with cattle. A large bull statue sat in the middle of the front yard.

Lucinda parked out front. "It's been too long since I've been here. Emile always has something interesting to say. He knows pretty much everyone."

I got out and walked up the steps. Two large wooden doors greeted me. On the front was a bull's head surrounded by swords with the name Safreo at the top.

A fancy manor with the family crest on the doors, some roses by the porch, and perfectly trimmed grass. Of course

144

nobles' beauty standards would extend to their houses and not just their looks. I wonder if he has a fancy, shiny car too. I don't see one.

The door opened wide. Emile stepped back and waved his hand to invite us in. "Ah, glad to see you all. Come in. It's been getting rather chilly out there." He led us into a cozy lounge with a beige and orange color scheme. "How was the trip? I see you're using the car again."

"They allowed me to drive it," Lucinda said with a smile.

I glared at her. "Only after you stole it..."

"For a trip into town. You were with me. You didn't try to stop me."

"Not surprising," Emile said. "You do have impeccable memory, Lucinda."

"Thank you."

He glanced at his watch. "Ahh, dinner should be about ready if you lovely ladies would care to join me."

Looks like a cozy place. Warmer than the Mourlonet manor. Fewer portraits and achievements, more animal paintings and travel posters.

Emile gestured toward one of the larger paintings. "My parents were keen on having Bethany and I learn fine art skills. Neither of us were any good musically, so we ended up painting." He gestured toward a row of cattle paintings along the wall. "These were our best. Bethany was better with colors."

"They all look great," I said, following him into the dining room. "My parents didn't really care what Viv and I learned, as long as we worked hard on it."

He sat at the head of the table. "We have slow roasted beef, potatoes, and vegetables from a local garden. Don't worry about perfect etiquette."

"Fine with me," Lucinda said, grabbing her fork.

This looks great. I'm glad Emile isn't worried about being proper. I wonder if his parents would have been stricter. Lorena is still sitting perfectly poised, moving with calm regality.

"Did you have any hobbies?" Emile asked, looking at me.

"I tried to learn how to write short stories. Vivienne said I was good, but I never really kept up with it. She was glad to learn any skill that involved her meeting new people."

"She was the social one?"

"Yes. Whenever we went out or had guests, I would usually stand back and let Viv do all the talking. Now I have Luce for that, though my glares don't seem to have any effect on her."

"Luce takes glaring as a challenge to up her antics."

"I've noticed."

"Glad you were able to find a good family."

"Are your parent's home?" Lorena asked.

"No," he responded. "They are meeting with a realtor. Hopefully they finally pick a place."

"Where are they moving to?"

"Either Britain or Italy. They haven't decided yet. I am curious, have you ever considered moving out of the manor?"

"Unlikely."

"I assumed as much, though you got along with your parents far better than me and Bethany."

"Your sister?" I asked.

"Yes. She moved out at the first opportunity she had. Married a train conductor. Practically flew out of the house."

Lucinda looked down at her plate. "Lucian wanted to move out and start a family, have a place to ourselves… What?"

"You having a child is a bit frightening," I said. "I can hardly deal with one of you." *Suspicious… Why does she look nervous all of a sudden?*

"Did your parents know about them?" Emile asked Lorena.

"Yes," she responded. "They weren't as subtle as they intended."

"Think your parents would have allowed their union?"

"They both loved her dearly."

"I'm a catch." Lucinda leaned back and winked at me.

"How is business?" Lorena asked.

"Never better," Emile answered. "My sister's involvement with the transportation industry has helped.

My father recently invested in better heaters for the barn. Cows are happier than ever."

Lucinda sat up with excitement. "Can we see the calves?"

"Of course. Is everyone done?"

Lorena nodded. "The food was spectacular, Emile."

He smiled. "Nothing but the best for fine ladies such as yourselves."

Lucinda sprinted out the door.

"My, she has energy," Emile said.

"Too much sometimes," I added, following him out.

"Must be an efficient worker."

"No one folds laundry faster."

"I bet." He opened the barn door. "Ladies first."

The barn was large, made of sturdy light brown wood. The floor was covered in fresh straw. Brown and white cows stood strewn about, munching on fresh hay.

"It's pretty warm in here," I said.

Emile pet one of the larger cows. "Brand new electric heaters. These cattle are practically high-class themselves with how spoiled they are. Lottie here won't even drink water unless it's the right temperature."

"They deserve it for being so cute," Lucinda said, hugging a calf.

"They are far too adorable."

"Foals are clumsier. Definitely more entertaining to watch."

"I beg your pardon," he said with a grin. "Calves are twice as adorably clumsy."

"The foals have longer legs."

"Are you insinuating that foals are cuter?"

"No, I think the calves are cuter."

"Smart girl. Lorena, which do you think?"

"Foals."

"El?"

"Foals."

"Well, we are thoroughly divided it seems."

I stepped closer. "You'll just have to see for yourself next time you come over."

"That I shall." He peered out the door. "Looks like it might rain again. You might want to get back home before the roads get slick. I know that one hill can be tricky."

Lorena shook his hand. "Thank you for the invitation. Your home is always a delight to visit."

"And you three are always a delight to see. Allow me to walk you back to your car. It will give me a chance to ask a few more gossip-worthy questions."

"Alright."

"I assume you still aren't going to tell me who has caught your eye?"

Lorena smiled. "No."

"Figured as much. How about you two?"

Lucinda grinned. "Nothing new with me."

"El?"

"Nothing going on with me, either." *Could you not glare at me so obviously, Luce?*

Emile opened the car door for Lorena. "All three of you, single, as beautiful as you are? Shocking." He smiled and tipped his hat. "Do have a lovely evening."

Lorena nodded. "You as well, Emile."

Great, that feeling is back. Am I jealous? Worcard is noble, someone who clearly has an eye on Lorena. She did say she was interested in someone when we were at the party, but we avoided him when we got there so it probably wasn't him... I don't know, I still feel off knowing he's going to be coming over to have tea. Do nobles ask each other out over tea? Is that some rich person thing? Stop overthinking this, El. She doesn't seem all that interested in him. Just relax and think about how cute the calves were. Luce is still rambling about them.

-

"Eleanora, you okay?" Lucinda asked, parking next to the manor. "You've been quiet since we left Emile's."

I got out of the car. "Just tired, I guess. We should see how Joey is doing. I'm sure Eve has had her running around all day."

Lorena got out of the car and headed inside.

Luce walked up to me, glaring. "You're sulking, aren't you?"

There's no hiding things from anyone in this house.
"Maybe, a little..."

"Is it about Worcard's obvious crush on Lorena?"

"Yes..."

"Don't worry, she's just being polite."

"Are you sure?"

"Yes. You can always ask her what she thinks of him."

"I guess."

"Stop being so negative or I'll tell Evangeline about your crush."

"Evangeline would definitely tell Lorena."

"If she doesn't know already."

She probably does, with some of the comments she's been making lately...

"It's cold in here."

"The heat is out," Mary Ann said, walking by. "We have to wait on a new part to be delivered. Make sure everyone has extra blankets. No tying blankets to the dogs, Lucinda." She glared at her and walked out.

"Fine..." Luce got close to me and whispered. "She didn't say not to put shirts on them... They get cold, too."

I smiled. "Do we still have the shirts we put on them last time?"

"They're in the lower storage room, on the extra chairs. I'll grab them and meet you in the lounge."

"I'll see where your mother went." *Sneak down the hall... Check for Mary Ann... She's in her room, dusting off cat statues. Perfect. The dogs should be down this hall in the lounge. Okay. Good so far.*

"Are we clear?" Luce asked, walking in.

"Yes, Mary Ann should be busy for a while."

"We can always go hide again if she decides to wander by."

"It's too cold to go in the tunnel."

"Where do you suggest?"

"The kitchen pantry."

"Then we would have snacks. That's much better."

"Something I learned from my sister. Always have a hiding spot by the food. That way we can hide as long as we need."

"She must have been the queen of hide and seek."

"She was."

Chapter 16

Michella stood in the barn, arguing with Evangeline about who was wearing better overalls. They looked the same to me: plain dark denim with large pockets and firm stitching. *I guess Michella's do look a little newer*, I thought, watching her sign something before shoving Eve into one of the stalls.

"Ready for your lesson, El?" she asked, turning toward me.

"Yes."

"Get your wild beast ready."

Bellezza stood at the door to her stall, ready to go. "We have a visitor today," I said, getting her saddle situated. "He's nice, but kind of boring. He's also interested in Lorena. I guess I'm feeling a little outclassed."

I'd noticed myself rambling to her at times, getting out my frustrations. Bellezza was good at keeping me on track, nudging me whenever I'd ramble too much. The fact that she couldn't spill my secrets was also a plus. Anything Lucinda heard would be in everyone's ears by the end of the day. I didn't know if she had mentioned my feelings to Lorena, though if she hadn't, I assumed it would only be a matter of time, so it was safer just telling Bellezza.

"You're going to do it, aren't you?" I said, staring into the horse's eyes. She nodded her head. "Of course you are." I hopped on, holding tight to the reins as she sprinted for the gate. Her legs kicked up, folding back as we flew over. She raced around the barn in perfect rhythm, a routine I was starting to get used to. I had no doubt that horse could win competitions without a rider. She learned all the routines far faster than I did.

"Alright," Michella said, watching us jump back into the arena. "Now that you've got your jitters out, let's work on posture. After that we'll go over some low jumps."

Okay. Keep with the rhythm, sit up straight, watch where I'm going. Riding is all about communication...at least, it's supposed to be. Most of the time it's just Bell doing whatever she wants and assuming all of my commands are merely suggestions. Come to think of it, it's a bit like how I am with Luce and Viv...

"Focus, El."

"Right." *Prepare for the jump, move with Bell, and don't fall off. So far so good. She's going a bit faster today. We did miss a lesson this week.*

"Better, now go for the medium jump. Remember not to tense up too much when she jumps."

It's not her jumping, it's the adrenaline mixed with the sound of hooves. It still gets to me a little, though not as bad. I wonder if it will ever fully go away, or if I'm going to be a paranoid old woman still afraid of thundering sounds.

A crash echoed from the smaller barn. Michella rushed toward an escaping group of goats. "Pete, you menace, get back in there!"

Of course it's Pete. That animal refuses to be contained. I watched him run around in circles, staying just far enough away from her to not get caught. *Little troublemaker is doing it on purpose. Clever thing.* I turned Bellezza back toward the barn.

"How do you think we did today?" I asked. She let out a chuff and shook her head. "Yeah, me too."

"You're improving well. Have you thought about doing competitions?"

I looked up to see Lorena standing next to the barn. *How long has she been there?* "I'm not sure. Seems a little too stressful for me, though I'm sure Bellezza would love it."

"She knows the routines. One of the easiest horses to jump, though you're not quite on the same page. You need to add more energy to match hers."

"I wasn't as focused today."

"Anything in particular?"

Yes, but I don't want to say it. "How was tea?"

"Fair. He did most of the talking. He isn't as infuriating as most of the others."

"Was he just as indirect today? Yesterday he was tiptoeing around the topic of you two getting together."

"His conversations are like a dance. He slowly works his way into information, making intelligent evaluations and easing into topics. He's patient and careful."

"At least he isn't a Botlig."

"True. Unfortunately, they will be arriving soon. They insisted on making a business plan before the party."

"Are they staying the night?"

"Yes."

"Fantastic," I said sarcastically.

"I'd like you to be a part of the meeting. You know more about the production of our new wine."

"I'm sure I'll be ignored as always."

"Don't be afraid to be firm with them."

"Fine, I'd hate to leave you to deal with them on your own."

"Merci, ma belle."

One sentence and I'm a blushing mess. Viv would be teasing me right now.

Michella returned out of breath. "Damn thing is too smart for his own good."

"Why don't you change the latch?" I suggested.

"We did, four times."

I laughed. "I'd honestly prefer chasing him around over meeting with the Botligs."

"They here for another meeting?"

"Yes. Lorena wants me to join. Could you put Bell away for me?"

"Sure. Good luck."

I turned toward Lorena. "Should I change first? I'm covered in horse hair."

"They won't notice."

"Because they barely acknowledge my existence?"

"They don't think workers are worthy of their time. They won't care what you wear, but if you are firm and knowledgeable, they will care about what you say."

"They haven't so far."

"You aren't exactly the boldest person." She opened the manor door. "But you are worthy of respect nonetheless."

Back inside. It's still cold. The furnace must still be broken.

Miss Evarchest met us in front of the meeting room. "Ready?"

"No."

"Neither am I. Let's get this over with." She walked in and stood at the end of the table. "The party tomorrow will be focused on the release of our new wine, Mourlonet Rosan. We will hand out samples sparingly to keep people intrigued while sustaining its rarity."

"Perfect timing," Mr. Botlig said. "This estate has been long overdue for a party. We should start selling immediately after."

"We're still preparing further batches. At the moment we have two barrels. That should be enough."

"Two barrels? Merely two? That will not be sufficient for sales. Our esteemed guests will want first class access to the finest new product. They will not want to wait."

"It is more than sufficient for the event. Once we make more, we will be providing this to only our most esteemed buyers."

"We have new clients overseas who will wish to be first in line, not to mention the collectors. The highest of families wait for nothing, including ours."

"Wine takes time. We have to use barrels that were intended for Sanguine or Rose. Those stocks will be lower. We need to have time to compensate."

"We need results."

I spoke up. "They will be ready in two weeks."

Mr. Botlig turned toward me and raised an eyebrow. "How many?"

"Four barrels."

"We only transport the finest goods. No imperfections are allowed."

Miss Evarchest glared at him. "None will be received."

"Are you certain?" He turned toward Lorena. "You fired your best worker with decades of experience, and for what, exactly?"

Miss Evarchest interjected. "Unfair treatment of new hires. We value loyalty. If our head of production is verbally abusing workers, they won't give an ounce of care toward assuring quality."

"He knew quality. Perhaps the other workers were to blame."

"Are you questioning our knowledge of our own employees?"

"Clearly."

"Perhaps you should focus on your own company matters and not attempt to dictate our affairs."

"I need to make sure our most profound business partners aren't slipping. If you cannot keep proper staff, then we are at risk as well."

"There is no risk. We fired one man. Production has been excessively smooth since."

They are arguing over something that isn't even a problem. Great. I don't know how Lorena deals with them so well. I know my parents wouldn't put up with all this yelling. At least they don't get anyone else involved. Just a free show for the rest of us... Wait, where did Lorena go? Maybe I can sneak out as well. They aren't looking this direction.

I closed the door, feeling a wave of relief as the sounds of arguing muffled. A flash of light struck the room followed by the cold rumble of thunder. The storm seeped into the manor through a nearby window. Rain violently tapped against the glass. The sound faded as I made my way further into the old mansion. *It remains unmoved; unconcerned; still. Simply existing while people argue within it, and the harsh storm beats down onto it... I'm starting to sound like Lorena.*

159

The tall dark oak doors of the library stood before me. The doorknobs curled out of the mouths of golden lions. Normally this room was enchanting. Large, extravagant chandeliers would expose the titles of thousands of books to curious eyes. Now it sat still and quiet, matching the tone of the mansion around it. A silhouette sat in the windowsill across from me, staring out at the storm. My footsteps left soft echoes as I walked up to her.

"Do we ever get what we desire?" she asked, continuing to stare out at the storm. "Every time we reach our goal, it ends, and a new goal is created. We reach our desires only to feel a moment of achievement, then to be cast back out into a new task we must complete. We repeat this continuously—at least, most of us do. In that way we are predictable."

Silence filled the room for a moment. I stepped closer, looking out at the raging storm. It would have been freezing back home. The leak in the kitchen roof, the hole in the closet wall from when the donkeys got out and decided to cause a ruckus.

"Are they still at odds?" she asked, breaking the silence.

"Yes. I got tired of their bickering."

"Come, sit with me. The storm outside is far more entertaining than the one within."

I sat across from her in the windowsill. The trees swayed with the wind as the dreary clouds raced above them. Ever so slowly, the world outside grew darker as the night began to take hold. I turned and watched her for a minute. The shadows of the rain reflected onto her. Ghosts of water droplets ran down her face.

"Bartren is due to arrive tomorrow," she said.

"Hopefully he will help ease their constant arguing. He's much better company."

"I do enjoy his demeanor. He's respectful."

"He also doesn't try to pester you with questions and propositions like the others do."

"He is content with my behavior, like you." She got up and reached out with her hand. "We should prepare for bed. We have a long day tomorrow."

The hallway was getting dark. Bickering emerged from the conference room. "They will probably be up for a while," I said, walking to the stairs.

"Eleanora, would you stay with me tonight? It's hard to sleep in the cold."

I paused and stared at her for a moment. *Stay...with her?* "Of course. I'll change and meet you there." *Did that...actually just happen? Lucinda is going to explode.* Another rumble of thunder rattled the windows. *Right, stop standing around. Okay...be sneaky, don't want Luce finding out, she's going to pester me about this later. Walk to my room... Get changed... Peek out the door... No Luce, good. Carefully tip toe to Lorena's room... And Mary Ann is in the hallway... Great.*

"Evening, El."

"Evening, Mary Ann."

She looked me over. "Going for a stroll before bed?"

"I know you know. You have that grin on your face that says you know exactly why I'm here in my nightgown."

She chuckled and tapped my shoulder. "I'll wait to tell Luce until the morning. I know she'll be pestering you about it."

"Thanks."

"You at least tried to be sneaky. Luce was always too fast. She would try and run down the hall to not get caught. I'd say this tactic is more successful."

"You still know everything."

"Of course. I'm a mother. Have a good night, dear."

That went well, now I just have to knock...

"Come in."

Open the door. There she is. Her nightgown is cute, grey with lace around the waist. Makes her look even paler. Oh, I'm staring... I looked away, taking a deep breath. "I heard Mondair was going to be making a foreign dish tomorrow for dinner."

She waved for me to join her on the bed. "Yes, we got a shipment in from the coast earlier today. It should be quite extravagant. He does like to show off for guests."

"I just hope Emile doesn't try to dance with me again. He really isn't good at it."

"He is quite interested in you."

"He's a sweet man, tries so hard to impress me, and I'm not even noble."

"Nobility does not mean anything to him. Besides, you're definitely worthy of a noble."

My cheeks burned. "How about Worcard? Do you hope to see him there tomorrow?"

"Not particularly. I have different interests."

"Different?" I asked, moving closer to her on the bed. My mind filled with Luce's encouragements. *Be bold, just talk about it.*

"I would rather find a partner more like you."

"Like me?"

"I do enjoy your company." She placed her hand onto mine.

"Lorena..." My words trailed off in nervous anticipation. *Say something, El...*

She gently placed her other hand onto my cheek, smiling as my eyes widened. "Eleanora?"

"Yes?"

"What are your interests?"

I grabbed her hand, entwining our fingers. "You."

She leaned forward, kissing me. I wasn't sure how long we were there, her arms wrapped around me, my hands gently grasping her face. *Everything is quiet... It's just us. She likes me. She likes me.*

Lorena pulled back, allowing me to rest my head on her shoulder. *That was overwhelming. Her hair smells like flower petals and wine. Appropriate.*

She ran her fingers through my hair. "We should get some rest for tomorrow, darling."

Darling. She called me darling. I get to cuddle with her, kiss her. We're together now. This is home.

The rain continued tapping on the windows, though now it was just the rain. No more hooves and cries I never heard, just cold droplets against glass.

Chapter 17

Still raining. Grey and cloudy. Wonder what time it is. I probably have to get up soon. Wait, those aren't my curtains. Right, I'm in Lorena's room. I wonder if she's still asleep. We're together now... We're together now! I have a girlfriend. A very fancy girlfriend. How did I get here? Maybe I don't want to think about that. Oh, I think she's moving. Must be waking up.

Lorena sat up. "Did you sleep okay?"

"Yes. It's not the first time I've shared a bed. Viv would climb into mine whenever it would get too cold. We only had the fireplace for heat."

She smiled. "Lucian would sneak into my room when he would get scared. Our cousins would try to frighten him with stories of a ghostly monster hiding in the vines."

"Did it scare you too?"

"It did, until Father took us out to the vineyard one night on his old grey horse, Magnificent. Lucian and I had our eyes closed, scared that if we saw the monster, it would get us. Father told us to look up instead. The stars were so bright that night. We sat there for a while, naming the stars, listening to the animals in the barn. He told us, 'Most things that are real you can see. The stars, the moon, the sun, and all that is around us. There are some things that we cannot see, some things we don't know about. We learn and discover every year, so I won't tell you that there are no creatures that live in the vines. Instead, I will encourage you to look for them. See what animals hide in the leaves, which ones like the fruits. Knowing what is around will help the fear fade.' I haven't been afraid since."

"So you inherited your philosophical side from him?"

"He was always spouting something deep. I always wanted to learn how to talk like him when I was young. People loved hearing him speak. He could grab anyone's attention with his profound wisdom."

"You always have my attention, no matter how you speak."

She leaned forward and kissed my cheek. "Thank you, darling. Mary Ann should be in soon with our attire for the day."

"Right, the party." *Four slow knocks. Definitely Mary Ann.*

"Come in."

Mary Ann entered with a couple of dresses in her arms. One was a dark red with a black grape vine pattern around the waist. The other was black with a red grape leaf design around the waist. "Your outfits are ready." She placed the dresses at the foot of the bed. "I thought you two might want to match today."

"Why would you think that?" I asked with a smile.

"No particular reason, my lady." A wide grin crossed her face. "Do you need anything?"

My lady...

"No," Lorena answered. "We will be down shortly."

"Very well." She nodded and stepped out.

Lorena stood and reached out. "Come here. I'll help you put it on."

"It's fancier than I'm used to."

"It's simpler than it looks."

"I'd like to check on the barrels this morning, make sure everything is the right temperature. I'm sure Bartren will want to 'inspect' the product."

"Sad to see him drowning his sorrows. At least he has good taste."

"She was a lovely woman."

"She was."

"Alright, it's on." She pulled me closer for a kiss. "Don't be gone too long."

Cazzo...it's going to be hard to focus on the party now. I'm going to have to try and not stare at her with lovestruck eyes all day. I don't think she's going to want the guests to know. I honestly wish I could hide in the winery all day and rant to Anthony about my feelings.

Anthony stood in the center of the barrel room with a large smile on his face. "Good morning. We got the example Rosan bottle from the company." He held out a pristine purple bottle.

"Looks perfect."

"We'll have Lorena take a look after the event. If she approves, then we'll place the order."

"Sounds good. How's the new batch?"

"Seventy-four degrees precisely."

"Good. Everything going smooth?"

"Perfectly. You won't need to worry about us out here. Have fun with your party."

"I'm not really looking forward to dealing with another crowd."

"You're a worker. They probably won't pay you much mind, unless word gets out..."

"What?"

"Lucinda was by earlier. Seems a new rumor is floating around the manor."

I blushed. "What sort of rumor?"

"Someone was in the lady's room last night. Know anything about that?"

I smiled. "I might... It was very cold. The heat is broken."

"Never thought our lady would be swept up by a commoner." He nudged my shoulder. "Almost thought she was going to stay single forever with how many suitors she's turned down."

I leaned back against one of the empty barrels. "I didn't exactly imagine getting involved with a noblewoman."

"Think your parents would be proud or disappointed that you got involved with a competing wine family?"

"They would have welcomed her without question. My sister would have gladly helped set me up with Lorena, to be honest. She was almost as encouraging as Lucinda."

He put a comforting hand on my back. "Their girl's going far."

"Thanks, Anthony. I'd better get back to the manor. Don't let Bartren open any of the newer barrels."

"I'll do my best."

People should be arriving soon. It's easier to traverse the garden when Evangeline isn't there. Glad Lorena gave her the day off. Wouldn't want guests getting hit in the face with flying plants.

"Is everything on schedule?" Lorena asked, meeting me by the main entrance.

"Yes. Anthony arrived early this morning to make sure we didn't get behind."

"Good."

"First guest is here," Mary Ann said, fixing her dress. She walked up to the door, ready to greet. I stood to the side of the stairs next to Miss Evarchest. She took a long drink from her glass, her face plastered with a cross between excitement and annoyance. Lorena stood at the base of the stairs, watching the guests enter. All wore respectable attire: suits, dresses, and the occasional foreign garb.

Emile walked in wearing his typical top hat and grey suit. His face shifted into a grin as he noticed me.

"Captivating as always." He reached out, gently kissing the back of my hand.

"How have you been, Emile?"

"Rather well, actually. My parents moved to Italy. Finally have the manor to myself." He leaned closer, whispering, "I definitely didn't throw a party with our servants after they left."

I smiled. "Of course you didn't."

"Did the meeting go well yesterday?"

"Endless bickering. Nothing was accomplished."

"Not surprising. The Botligs must make their opinions known."

"I can't wait until they leave."

"When is that?"

"One more night."

"Well, we will just have to avoid them until then."

"Any suggestions?"

"They like attention, so if we avoid the center of the room, we should be fine."

The Botligs were quick to hound the attention of new arrivals. They stood in the entryway to the ballroom, greeting everyone with arrogant smiles and sharp, judging eyes.

Most of the evening was spent watching small groups shuffle around, chatting about business. They would show up in their best outfits to every event, ready to sweet talk whomever they could into deals and propositions followed by the typical competitive bragging. New vehicles, profits, and marriage proposals. It all sounded the same after a while.

"People seem to be enjoying it," Joey said, setting down her tray of glasses.

"How many bottles have we gone through?" I asked.

"Twenty. Mr. and Ms. Endfarth have had several glasses each. They're far too sneaky."

"How's Alanna doing?"

"Good. I'm so glad Emile let us borrow her for the event. Always good to have extra hands...speaking of."

Alanna's short, brown-haired figure appeared in front of us. "The Botligs have some sort of announcement planned," she whispered.

"About what?" I asked.

"Not sure. Their chauffeur wouldn't tell me."

The youngest Botlig parted from the group. Nicolas Botlig the Fourth. Certainly the quietest of his family. High expectations followed him every second of his life. His parents stared with a grin, practically glowing with excitement as he approached Lorena. "I have a proposition, or rather a heartfelt quest I must peruse." His smile grew as he stepped closer, reaching out his hand. "Would you do the honors of becoming my partner?"

Did he really just ask her out?

The room went quiet. Mary Ann stood across from me, shaking her head. Joey had a hand over Luce's mouth, trying to keep her quiet.

Lorena kept her calm demeanor. "I will have to decline. As of last night, I am no longer available."

He looked surprised and a little worried. "Really? Who beat me to it, then?"

She looked back at me, took my hand, and gently pulled me to stand next to her. My heart started racing. *Damn she's bold.*

Ms. Botlig looked cross. "You can't be serious."

"I am."

"Your name will be tarnished," Mr. Botlig said, stepping forward. "Pairing with a commoner, a woman with whom you cannot produce an heir."

"That is none of your concern."

"My family only does business with the noblest of companies. I will not continue our agreement if you continue this outrageous action."

"Then I will comply and terminate our contract."

"You..."

Lorena turned. "Lucinda?"

"Yes, my lady?"

"Escort them out."

"Very well."

Everyone's eyes are on me now... At least no one else seems too bothered. Most of them just look entertained. Okay, people are returning to their chatter. Eyes are turning away. Everything's fine.

Emile walked up to me. "That was unexpected."

"Yes..."

"I hadn't known you were interested in Lorena. Bit of a scandal, don't you think?" He smiled.

"I didn't know she was going to announce it like that..."

"It was rather entertaining, to be honest. The look on the young lad's face was priceless."

"Are you upset at all? I know you were trying to court me yourself."

"Not at all. Anyone would be lucky to have her hand."

Mary Ann walked up to us with a tray of wine glasses. "How are you enjoying the party?"

Emile took a glass. "It's wonderful, Mary Ann. How long have you known about Lorena and El?"

She smiled. "Honestly thought they would have started dating sooner."

"Really?" He looked back at me with a smile. "Always go to the head maid for information. They hear everything."

"I'll keep that in mind next time I visit your estate."

He chuckled. "I've clearly said too much." His eyes wandered around the room. "Now, where has that lady of yours gone?"

I turned toward the lounge. Lorena had vanished.

"I believe I saw her head into the kitchen," Mary Ann said.

"Why don't we join her?" Emile suggested. "These fancy pants crowds bore me."

We followed Mary Ann down the hallway and quietly snuck into the kitchen. Lorena leaned against the counter with a glass of wine in hand.

"Not a fan of real estate talk?" Emile asked.

"Donotest won't shut up," Lorena responded.

"Rather enjoyed your little argument earlier. The Botligs needed to be put down a few pegs."

I stood next to her. "It was a bit of a surprise."

She spoke, "I thought the direct approach would be best."

"I'm glad few people challenge your decisions."

"The Mourlonet family has commanded respect for many years," Emile said. "They have mastered the look of confident absolution."

I looked into Lorena's deep, dark brown eyes. "And the look of beauty."

She smiled and gently grabbed my hand. "Beauty worthy of your own."

"How did Worcard react?" Emile asked.

"I'm not sure," I answered. "I didn't see him much after he arrived."

Mary Ann spoke up. "He looked entirely unamused. Left after the Botligs."

"Not too surprising," Emile said. "Are you worried at all about your company, Lorena? The Botligs have a surprising number of contacts, considering how annoying they are."

"No," she responded. "I already have another shipping deal lined up. Spoke with Ms. Thaws this morning about a contract."

"That woman is clever. She must have seen this coming a mile away, especially with the gossip her maids get into."

I grabbed Emile's arm. "Since you're here, how about we head to the barn to settle our debate? The foals are looking cute as ever."

"Wonderous idea, my dear. Lead the way."

Chapter 18

"Tired?" Anthony asked, watching me walk in.

"I don't even know what time we went to bed."

"You were still chatting in the barn when we left the winery."

"We were there to convince Emile that foals are cuter than calves."

"Did he agree?"

"Instantly caved when he saw the twins."

"Most people do. Have much to drink?"

"Not too much... Lorena had to help me up the stairs a little..."

"Spend another night with her?"

"Maybe..."

"I heard about last night's scandal. Can't believe Nicolas tried asking Lorena out. Wish I would have been there to see the look on those arrogant assholes faces when he was denied."

"He couldn't believe it. I almost had a heart attack myself. Honestly thought she would want to keep it a secret, at least for a little while."

"She's not scared of the pompous rules of the higher class. She does what she wants, better no one gets in her way."

I walked up to a stain on the floor. "What happened?"

"Bartren got into a fight with Pete."

"In here?"

"Not sure how that goat keeps getting in. Bartren ended up getting his bottle knocked out of his hand. All the barrels are okay."

"Sounds like you had just as wild of a night."

"Bartren was ready to help us defend the wine."

"How was he? I didn't see him at the party."

"Already drunk when he got here. Shame what he's turning into. The tussle with the goat did help liven his spirits for a while."

"That's good."

"So, are you still going to be working here, or is she going to move you to higher responsibilities?"

"I'll still be here."

"I remember when you first showed up. A quiet, uncertain girl with nowhere to go, and surprisingly knowledgeable in the art of winemaking."

I smiled. "You were always so kind. One of my dearest friends."

"Still now that you're a lady?"

"Always, Anthony."

-

"How long were we dusting for?" I asked, setting down my cloth. I get that we have to make everything as clean and high quality as possible, but that's so many bottles. No wonder they are so expensive. Each one gets a thorough wipe-down before being placed in the crate. They're treated just as well as the rich people that drink them."

"Quality is agonizing," Anthony responded.

The wall felt cold on my back. The faint memory of the barn, Viv's shoulder against mine, and the wind. For a moment, I felt like I was in both places at once.

"Glad we have heat in here," he said, leaning back next to me. "It's starting to get icy outside."

I smiled. "The barrels would turn into giant popsicles."

He laughed. "Yeah, they would."

"My sister and I snuck into the wine shed when we were...eight, I think? We stole one of the bottles and hid it in a bush outside, wondering if it would freeze into a wine popsicle. Our own bright idea of how to get more profits."

"Every child assumes the world needs more popsicles."

"Exactly."

"Did it work?"

"No, it didn't get that cold. Dad made us put it back."

Anthony grinned. "My brothers found an alligator popsicle once."

"A what?"

"We found a small alligator, only about a foot long, stuck in the ice. We had an unusually cold winter. My brothers spent an hour trying to get it out of the lake. We ran back home to show it off. Mother almost fainted."

"You got into more trouble than I did."

"I was a pretty calm kid, let my brothers get into all the trouble for me. We lived next to a big swamp. They were always daring each other to swim out to a fallen tree without getting eaten by anything. One day, Vinny came back missing a couple of fingers after swimming into an alligator. Never stopped him from going back in the water. They still do that every time we all get together. I like to sit back and have a glass of our famous Sanguine wine and enjoy the entertainment from the dock."

"Way more daring than we were." I looked up at the ceiling. "Vivienne and I used to do this...lean back against the cold bricks outside the barn and just listen. It was nice after working all day. We had a spot behind the back corner that looked into the woods. That side didn't get as much wind, so we were able to stay dry during rainstorms."

"I'm sorry about what happened. I know I'd miss my brothers if anything happened to them."

"Viv used to make all the decisions. I'd just go along for the ride. It's weird not having her pulling me in one direction or the other."

"Try having four pulling you in different directions. That was a wild ride. My brothers couldn't agree on anything most of the time, so they were always trying to convince me who to help with their latest adventure. I do kind of miss that."

"You're always welcome to join in on Lucinda's adventures."

"She'd outmatch my brothers, no problem." He looked at the clock. "Better get going or I'll become a popsicle on my way home. See you tomorrow."

I grabbed my coat and followed him out the door. The wind kicked up. *I wish that tunnel was heated.* Alanna, Josephine, and Luce stood in the kitchen, watching me walk in. Luce nudged my shoulder. "Just in time for your interrogation."

"Interrogation?"

"Spill. How'd it happen?"

"What?"

"You and Lorena."

"Oh, she couldn't sleep in the cold, so she invited me to stay with her. We ended up talking and...that's pretty much it."

"Great excuse."

"What's it like being with a noble? Alanna asked.

Luce was quick to answer. "Way more fun. The scandal, the rumors, the rush of feeling worthy of someone high-class. Loved every second of it. I was with Lucian before the accident."

"Does no one in this family want to be with another noble?"

"Most of the higher class are too far up their own asses to be interesting. We have personality and skill."

Joey looked at me with a nervous smile. "Did you...."

I threw a roll at her. "No. We just started dating. Keep your mind in your own bedroom." I looked back at Luce. "You're a terrible influence on her."

Luce winked at Joey. "In more ways than one. You don't have to worry about noise, since no one else lives in that hall besides her. The walls are pretty thick, so it still wouldn't be much of a problem."

"This coming from personal experience?" I asked.

"Maybe..."

Alanna looks so shocked. "Not what you expected?" I asked her.

"Not at all. This place is far more casual and less...demanding than I thought."

"Have anyone you're interested in?"

"No. Mother keeps trying to suggest men, but I'm honestly fine on my own for now."

Luce opened her mouth. I put a hand over it. "No, she's only here for one more day. You can keep your hands off of her."

"I wasn't thinking that!"

"Sure."

"I'm serious!"

"You're a serious flirt."

"You love me, El."

"I do."

Alanna blushed. "What is it with the women in this manor..."

Chapter 19

A few of the flowers kept their bright, colorful faces. I could imagine Evangeline giving them energetic pep talks. She would be the type of person to keep flowers blooming long past the first chill purely out of spite.

"Do you like the snow?" Lucinda asked, looking out the lounge window.

"From in here. It's beautiful, though I'm the not the biggest fan of the cold."

Mary Ann walked in accompanied by two taller gentlemen. Both had dark hair and simple black suits with red accents. She gestured toward them. "Lord Leo, and Lord Grigorio."

Lucinda leaned closer to me. "Lorena's cousins."

"Lucinda." Leo nodded at her then looked at me. "And you are?"

"Eleanora."

"Ah, Lorena's romantic interest." He reached out politely. "A pleasure to meet you. We were interested in examining the new wine. Mother has been quite intrigued by the story."

"Truly," Gregorio agreed. "We've heard the tale of how this came about. Frolont must have been furious."

Lucinda spoke. "He wasn't there. He was fired after getting drunk and hurting El."

"Oh, who has taken his position?"

"Eleanora and Anthony."

"Really?" He glared with a calculating look.

I guess the intimidating stares do truly run in the family.

Lorena walked in and gave Leo a welcoming hug. "Glad to see you."

Gregorio stood back and nodded. "Good to see you as well. We've had the pleasure of meeting your partner. Mother wasn't thrilled until we told her that it would put us in a better position. With you unable to sire an heir to the company, Leo and myself will be tasked with continuing the family name, shifting us into a more direct position in the family business."

Lucinda's got an anxious look on her face. Suspicious...

"I will welcome the assistance," Lorena said. "It has been difficult running it on my own."

Gregorio smiled. "Yes, it was devastating for us all. We will do whatever we can to help our family."

"You are more than welcome to be in charge of paperwork."

"I assumed you would say that. We will need to divert necessary papers to our estate, then you won't need to bother with it in the slightest. Your advisor will need to be informed."

"We will have a formal meeting with her before you leave."

"We won't be able to stay long. Mother has us attending business in England for a couple weeks. Our train departs early tomorrow morning."

Lorena turned toward Lucinda. "If you would call Evarchest for a meeting. Eleanora, please inform Josephine of their stay."

Leo sat down. "Have her bring some tea. The usual."

Somehow them being related to Lorena is making me more nervous than usual. I walked into the kitchen. Josephine was scrubbing off the counter. Mondair had already left. I was starting to wonder if he even existed. I couldn't recall ever seeing him in person, just heard the occasional mention or rumor about the chef who was never on time.

"Lorena's cousins are here."

She stopped and looked up at me. "Leo and Gregorio?"

"Yes."

"Tea?"

"The usual."

"Grab me a couple of the herbal blends, the ones to the left with the green paper."

I stared at the chaotic clutter of tea bags and boxes in the cupboard. They were supposed to be organized. The trick was looking at the handwriting. Evangeline's was scratchy and hard to read. We just had to guess what was in each blend, though hers were my personal favorites. Handpicked from the garden. The imports usually had fancy printed labels with bright colors, though only a few of them were in a language I could read, and the local teas were haphazardly tossed in between.

"Evarchest will be here after dinner," Lucinda said, walking in.

I handed Josephine the bags. "I'll be glad to not have to do all that paperwork anymore..." *Luce has that mischievous look on her face.* "What?"

"They don't come by all that often anymore. They were just as boring when we were kids. Would rather follow their mother around doing whatever they could to keep her happy. Never really wanted to play with Lucian and me. We used to tease them about it."

"If they're no fun, why are you so excited?"

"No reason in particular..."

"Luce..."

Josephine smiled. "She likes to cause extra trouble when they're around."

"What sort of trouble?"

"Shaking their champagne bottles, putting animals in their car, ambushing them in the garden with Evangeline, that sort of thing. She was allowed to get away with pretty much anything because of Lucian."

I glared at Lucinda. "What did you do this time?"

"Nothing...yet."

Mary Ann walked in. "Lucinda, I want you to keep away from our guests. El will keep an eye on you. You two go help in the barn today. Michella's got a sore leg."

Luce sighed and opened the door. "Fine..."

I followed her out. "You can't hide your love of trouble, Luce. Best to just give in and ask it out."

"I could probably seduce the god of chaos..."

Of course that's where she took that. "Do you even believe in that?"

"Percival said anything could be out there. Why not a hot god of chaos?"

"With my luck, you might just be the god of chaos."

"We'll then you've missed out. Could have gone for a chaos god, but no, you chose a beautiful lady."

"I'd choose Lorena over anyone."

"Cute."

"Morning, girls," Michella said, limping toward us.

"What happened?" I asked.

"Got distracted laughing at Eve and fell out of the loft."

"What did she do?"

"Got her foot stuck in a feed bucket." She chuckled. "She was fumbling around, falling on her ass. I couldn't help it."

"What do you want us to do?"

"Clean out and refill waters in the goat barn, then start cleaning out the stalls."

It reminds me of being back home. The donkeys were louder and more demanding, though not quite as problematic. Especially compared to that old goat. I glared through the door at the wobbly grey creature. *Has to stay in the barn all day because of his health. I know he's going to sneak into this stall and mess it up again when I'm done cleaning it. Finish a stall, start on the next one, then look back and see it completely destroyed again with old Twister sitting in the middle, munching on hay. He's just as much trouble as everyone else in this place.*

"I have to get more hay. Don't mess up any more stalls." *If I move quickly, I should be able to get it before he completely trashes everything. Ow. What? Why am I on the ground now?*

"Sorry," Lucinda said, getting off me. "Didn't see you..."

Pete pushed past us, running through the gate.

"Cazzo!" I yelled, chasing after. *This would be easier with Bellezza... Never mind, she'd just jump over him. Now I know how Michella feels. We have to get him out of the garden.* "Luce, go left... No, toward the lilies... Those aren't lilies... Wait, don't—" *And now she's on top of me again. This goat is just messing with us.*

Evangeline popped up out of nowhere and grabbed one of his horns. "Don't need more trouble from you, yah bag of fur." She wrapped an arm around him, hoisted him up, and carried him back to the barn.

Luce let out a tired breath. "That could have gone better."

"Or worse if someone had seen that. Wait..." *Why does it sound like someone's stirring tea*? I turned toward the covered bench. *Oh, of course Lorena and her cousins are right there. We're in so much trouble...*

Lucinda stood up. "It was an accident...this time."

"We fell through the gate," I added.

188

Gregorio sighed and put a hand over his face. Leo and Lorena smiled at each other, seemingly entertained.

"Did you finish your tasks?" Lorena asked.

"Almost," Lucinda answered. "I just need to finish filling waters."

"Very well, go and finish. El, come with us." She reached out and took my hand. "We will have you assist with paperwork, then I would like you to attend dinner with us."

I glared back at Lucinda. *Oh no, I'm not ready to spend the evening with her cousins.* She gave me an encouraging nod and headed back toward the barn. *Great... Now I have to try and impress two new nobles. Okay, remember to act confident, and not stare at Lorena the whole time... She does look stunning in that dress... Cazzo, this is hopeless.*

Evarchest welcomed us into the meeting room. "Good evening."

"Evening, Fran," Leo said, sitting down.

"I assume you have already discussed this?"

"Yes."

It's weird being in this room without any loud conflicts erupting. It's the first time I actually have a chance to look around. Was there always red floral wallpaper in here?

Evarchest grabbed a pen. "Lorena will remain head of the company. Gregorio and Leo will now hold executive titles." She scribbled a bold signature onto the paper. "You three sign. Eleanora, I'll have you sign as a witness, then

I'll get it to our business partners and legal records. Things go rather smoothly without the Botligs."

Lorena grabbed a pen. "I'm sure they would have had something to complain about."

"Their company has been faltering since we broke the contract. I'm curious how long until they come back, begging to reinstate it."

"They did not deserve their noble titles."

"Couldn't agree more." She grabbed the papers and smiled. "I'll get these to the post. Have a pleasant evening."

Okay, now for dinner with two new proper men dressed unreasonably well for a family visit... I can do this.

"Tell us about your family," Gregorio said, sitting at the dining table.

Lorena gave me a faint nod. *Confidence, right.* I straightened my posture and took a deep breath. "They started out making suits, then went into wine when they moved."

Leo smiled. "Interesting business change. Our family has always been involved with wine. The famed Mourellio family with their golden rose wines and unbeatable charm, and the Elonets with their blood red wines, prized Percheron horses, and their stern, respectable nature. Have you heard the story about how they united?"

"I haven't."

"Lorabella Mourellio, the family's golden daughter, stubborn as ever, decided to forge her own path. She had met Événor Elonet at a ball. Both were eager for greatness.

They planned to create a new sparkling wine. There were complications at first, and the wine was eventually split into two, what eventually became our Rose and Sanguine. The two achieved great accomplishments for both of their families and soon married, joining as Mourlonet. A bloodline of perfect regality, respect, and beauty."

I glanced over at Lorena. "No one more beautiful." *I said that out loud... Cazzo, El, why did you do that?* I looked back at the cousins. Leo gave me an approving nod. *Okay, they didn't seem to mind. Lorena's giving me such a loving smile. It's okay. No one cares that we're together. Everything's fine.*

Chapter 20

Light... Birds...? Did someone knock? I sat up, slowly opening my eyes. Lorena was asleep next to me, peacefully wrapped in the blankets. Another knock grabbed my attention. "Yes?"

Mary Ann opened the door. "The inspector is already here."

"It's not even seven. No one's in the winery yet."

"She didn't want to disturb workers."

"Okay. We'll be up soon." I turned toward Lorena, wrapping my arm around her. "Hey, we have a visitor to attend to."

"She knows her way around."

"Fine." I snuggled up close. "A few more minutes." I smiled and stared at the dresser against the wall. I no longer woke up, waiting to see a face that was gone. No longer expected the cold chill of a cracked window and the call of hungry donkeys. Now I woke up and was exactly where I wanted to be.

-

"Seriously?" I asked, walking into the kitchen.

Joey set down her tray. "What?"

"He already left?"

"Yeah."

"Still don't believe in the chef?" Luce asked, grabbing a cookie.

"I've never seen him," I responded. "He's always late, or just ran out before I walk in. I'm really starting to think you're all playing tricks on me."

"I swear he's real."

"I'll believe it when I see him."

"He does work at multiple places throughout the day. Rushes around a lot."

"Sure, whatever."

"I'm not lying!"

"I've lived here for how long, and I have never seen even a brief glimpse of him."

"He is always tired from going place to place all day. The curse of being a top chef. If only we could magically clone him. Then he could do two jobs at once, not have to rush around as much, and El would finally get to meet him."

"One of him is enough," Joey said.

"I think one of all of us is enough," I agreed.

"Yeah..." Luce grabbed another cookie and looked toward the floor with wide eyes.

I took a few steps closer. "Why have you been acting suspicious lately?"

"Yeah," Joey agreed. "You've been getting this new nervous look. Last time was when we were talking about what Leo and Gregorio would name their kids."

"She got weird when they were talking about Lorena and Lucian not continuing the family name…"

"I'm uh…" She gestured toward her stomach.

Joey's eyes widened. "Seriously? Have you told anyone else yet?"

"My mother."

I stepped closer. "Who have you been with recently, aside from Joey?"

"Just Lucian…a few days before…"

"Six months already?" Joey asked. "How? You don't look much different. Is that why you've been wearing looser clothes? Have you thought of names?"

"I kind of like Ophelia or Oliver. I didn't have the chance to ask Lucian if he had any particular names."

"Would they get your last name?"

"Probably. Me and Lucian weren't exactly official."

"Technically they would be a Mourlonet. Let's ask Lorena."

Luce raced up to the second story lounge, barging through the door dramatically. "I'm having your brother's kid."

Lorena didn't budge. "I know."

"What?"

"I overheard you rambling to yourself in the library the other day. Your mother has also been joyfully humming while she dusts."

"Fine, be so unreasonably clever." Luce plopped down on the couch.

"Would the child have her last name?" Joey asked.

Lorena looked up at Luce. "If you want. It is yours."

"I didn't know if they would count as a Mourlonet, or just a Fensworn. We weren't exactly official."

I sat down. "You really think she cares."

"No, just making sure."

"Do you have a name?" Lorena asked.

"Either Oliver or Ophelia. Do you know if Lucian had any names he wanted?"

"No. He didn't really speak of having children, though I'm certain it would be a pleasant surprise for him."

"Well, someone has to continue the family name. You two can't."

"True."

"Your aunt is going to be cross."

"She's cross with everything."

"You'll just have to have a really cute kid," I said. "One who she can't be mad at."

Joey looked up with excitement. "We can get them a tiny suit or dress. It would be so cute. She'd have to love them!"

Luce jumped up and grabbed Joey's arms. "I can get cool outfits from the odds market!" The two raced out the door.

"They have a few more months," I said.

"I know," Lorena responded. "Let them get out their excitement. It won't hurt to start preparing."

"The whole town's going to know soon. Think anyone will be upset?"

"The Botligs might try to use it against us, though I'm not worried. They don't have nearly as much respect as they used to."

"Everyone generally agrees that they suck."

"Even Worcard's mother."

I grabbed a nearby blanket and snuggled close. The fireplace danced shadows around the room, competing with the sunlight that peeked through the curtains.

"We each had our own spots to linger when we wanted to be alone," she said. "This was where we would meet when we were feeling social. Mother often came in after a lesson. Father and Lucian would take a break from business and join us. We would sit around the fireplace, listen to the radio, chat about our day, much like your morning gossip routine."

"Did they have a favorite spot? My father had his chair that only he was allowed to sit in."

"Mother and Father would sit on the couch to the right, Lucian always sat in the chair to the left, and I would be right here."

"It is pretty cozy here."

"More so with you, love." She kissed my forehead.

"I imagine we'd be sitting more proper if they were here."

"Most likely."

I smiled. "I can imagine what it would be like having you over for dinner, introducing you to my family. My father would try to dress his best and put up a show of politeness. Mother wouldn't act any different. She'd probably want to talk about profit comparisons or something. No doubt Viv would try to flirt with your brother."

"Sounds like our fathers would be competing for best dressed and most polite attitude. My mother would be more interested in learning what skills you have, education, and experience. Lucian would play along, but not show much interest."

"Sounds about right from what I know about them. Would I have had to ask them to be with you, like proper asking your father to date you?"

"No. Lucian got away with the least proper relationship he could have gone for. They would see us together and would be happy that you were at least from another wine family."

"Did they ever try our wine?"

"Yes, I believe they said it was fair, though not as bold as they would have preferred."

"My dad wanted the family logo on his grave. They were buried at the cemetery just outside of town. The one on the hill. Overlooks the train station and flower field. I'm sure they'd love the view."

She stood up. "Follow me."

"It's freezing."

"You can bring the blanket."

"Fine." *Not like I wouldn't follow her anywhere at this point. I wonder how the horses are doing. I should probably slip my boots on. I haven't had a chance to try the new coat Lorena got me. It's so soft. Perks of being with a noble.*

The snow clung to every tiny edge it could find along the manor's stone exterior, sharpening its appearance with stark white accents, hiding cracks and imperfections behind a festive cloak.

"What are you thinking, love?" Lorena asked, taking my hand.

"The snow never stuck to our old house or the barn. The eves were long enough to keep it off, though that didn't help the doors from freezing shut. We had this older donkey named Barrel. Smart thing. He would help push the barn door open when it would get cold and stiff." I reached for the barn door and watched it slide open with ease. "It's nice having properly functioning ones."

Bellezza let out a loud whinny and threw hay at us.

"Hey, stop that." I walked over to her stall, gently petting her head. "We can't jump right now, you're too clumsy in the snow. It's not safe." She snorted and shook her head. "Just going to sass me?"

"She's good at that," Lorena said. "She'll be like this until the snow melts."

"Perhaps we should invest in an indoor arena."

"She'd love that."

"Arkello doesn't seem to mind the weather."

"Few things bother him."

"He doesn't have to deal with difficult nobles all day. I'm sure the Botligs would bother him thoroughly."

She gently placed the reins over his head and climbed on. I got up behind her and wrapped the blanket around us. The cold chill battered my legs as we made our way out of the barn and toward the trees. The goats were mostly huddled in their barn, peeking out as we passed. The garden's once-colorful vibrance was replaced by twisting brown and green stems dusted in white. Evangeline stood outside the greenhouse in a thick lavender jacket, mumbling about the plants.

We're heading into the woods. I wonder where this leads. She did seem like she had a specific destination in mind. "I haven't been down this path before."

"Few traverse it."

A tall, thin metal gate appeared in front of us. Remnants of vines and branches twisted around it, holding it open. Arkello slowed down, holding his head low as we walked past a collection of gravestones. Most of the markers were made of marble. Some were old and worn. Vines wrapped around the ones closest to the gate. The snow covered them in a quiet blanket. A pair of small red birds danced around the markers, breaking the silent atmosphere. Arkello stopped, staring down at three white marble gravestones. Each one had grape vines carved around the edge and the family crest at the center painted gold. *Percival, Lillian, Lucian.*

I rested my head on her shoulder. "I wish I could have had the chance to meet them."

"Lucian would have disproved of you taking my attention away from business matters. He was almost more devoted to the company than father."

"The man fooling around with the maid?"

"He was hoping I'd pick up his slack. One of us fooling around would have been fine."

"Would they have hired me if they had lived?"

"Most likely. They were understanding of the less fortunate. You and I wouldn't have had to deal with all that paperwork."

"Sounds nice."

"Lucinda would be dragging you around for adventures less often if Lucian was still around."

"Did Lucinda tell you that I was falling for you?"

"Evangeline did, though by then I already knew."

"Lucinda was constantly encouraging me, spinning tales of sapphic romance and throwing flower petals at me."

"Few are quite as unique."

"Where does she get those from? I never see any missing from the garden."

"I don't know."

I looked back at the graves. "When did you last visit them?"

"The day after they were buried here. I didn't want to come here alone."

"I understand. I only visited the graveyard mine are buried at for their funeral. I had a lot to figure out."

"Would you like to visit them again?"

"Maybe after the snow clears a little. The hill's pretty steep."

We turned back toward the path, watching the birds circle around us. The snow had begun clinging to Arkello's mane, making it shine like the star-filled night sky. I closed my eyes and focused on the warmth of the blanket, the sound of hooves crunching through snow.

"What are you thinking?" Lorena asked.

"This reminds me of a time Viv and I tried sneaking to our friend's house with one of our uncle's horses. A bunch of us kids thought it would be fun to race them along the fence. We called it the Moonlit Run. We all met up late in the evening, trying to sneak through the woods without being caught. I'm surprised we actually got away with it. That was one of the funniest nights I can remember. Most of us didn't actually know what we were doing. One of the richer kids won, I think. I don't remember what her name was. She was very pretty. Rode across the field without a hint of hesitance. I was in awe. That was one of the moments I started realizing I was interested in women."

"El, honey...I won that race."

"What?"

"Lucian heard about the Moonlit Run from a friend of his. We snuck out with his horse, Crowmont. He was the fastest of our horses at the time. Lucian was happy just chatting with his friends while I competed. They were shocked when I raced past the other competitors. He spent the rest of the night bragging."

"You were... Well, I guess your beauty has always entranced me."

Chapter 21

Gold, white, bronze, and more gold, all of it unreasonably shiny. The plateware was almost more extravagant than the food sitting on it. The walls were a completely different scene. Large paintings and tapestries of all colors, from all countries. None had labels.

"They like to scope out people who are admiring the art," Emile said. "They'll talk your ear off about the history behind it, the personal lives of the artist, and the grand adventures they met them on."

"I still haven't met them," I said.

"The manor is currently owned by a group of sisters. Six in total. I believe Lady Anetta and Lady Augusta are here today. Perhaps you'll get the chance to meet them. They weren't at the last couple parties. The estate is still used for gatherings while they're gone. You'll know when you see them. They are quite unique. They own multiple companies all over the world, specializing in different beverages, wine, fernet, stout, port, whiskey, and a few others."

"Should we make our way to the usual spot?"

"Indeed."

My eyes were immediately drawn to the stairs as we left the entry hall. Two women descended in unreasonably shiny dresses. One was a brightly colored blue, green, and brown dress, fashioned in a peacock feather style. A string of light blue gems sat around her neck. Her eyes were soft brown, almost gold, nearly glowing against her dark skin. Her hair was medium length, held back with a golden hair clip. The second woman looked almost identical with a gold and blue dress of similar design and a golden feather necklace.

The pair walked up to us. "Ah, the Mourlonets, the Safreos, and you are?" the one in blue asked, looking at me.

"Eleanora Wintello," Lorena answered. "My partner."

"I bet that caused a commotion."

Emile smiled. "Entertainingly dramatic. Have you not heard?"

"No."

"Nicolas Botlig dared attempt to ask Lorena to be his partner during an event dedicated to the reveal of a new wine. Unbeknownst to him, Lorena and El had become a pair the evening before. Of course the Botligs were outraged. Poor Nicolas was just standing there confused, with no idea what to do while his parents argued. Lorena ended up breaking their contract and kicking them out. It was a fantastic evening from then on."

"Really? How exciting. Was Worcard there? He was attempting to court Lorena as well, if I remember correctly."

"He left shortly after the Botligs."

"I do wish I could have been there for that," the second woman said. "A perfectly good scandal to liven up the day."

"Have either of you seen him lately?"

"Haven't seen him in a while. He does seem to hang around less now that Lorena is unavailable."

"He's smart enough to not cause a scene like the Botligs. I am a bit relieved, though." He leaned closer for a moment. "He's dreadfully boring."

"Quite." The woman in the blue dress looked at Lorena. "At least you don't have to make up excuses to avoid him anymore."

"He wasn't too bad," Lorena said.

"Not as bad as Henscrook, or Mr. Kalatog!" She laughed. "Some of the men here are absolutely obscene." She looked back at me. "I actually pretended to be her consort once. An older man by the name of Richter Shodmyer was being a boorish sexist, wouldn't leave poor Lorena alone. I came down and quickly put him in his place. Lorena played along wonderfully. He was shocked but was too frightened to try and challenge me." She nudged Lorena's shoulder. "You were a terrible dancer."

"I did warn you," Lorena responded.

"It was still a thrilling night. I don't think I've seen him since."

"You were quite stern with him."

"He deserved it. Honestly, why do these fools act in such a way? I could never imagine treating a gorgeous thing like you so poorly. Some men are just obscene."

Emile smiled. "Then perhaps you should go for a woman yourself."

"Perhaps I shall."

The second woman glared toward the door. "Look who's here." She gestured toward an older couple who had just walked in. "Would you excuse us?"

"Of course," Emile responded, lifting his glass.

"Which was which?" I asked, watching them walk away.

"Augusta was in the green and blue dress, Anetta was gold."

"Got it."

"They don't introduce themselves. Most people already know who they are before they even enter a room. I only know which is which because I listen close at meetings. Doesn't help that all their names start with A."

"Really?"

"Anetta, Augusta, Alaia, Ariella, Aubree, and Adelaide."

"That's confusing."

"Very."

"How have you been, Emile?"

"Excellent. My sister came to visit—rather eager, in fact—after my parents left."

"Anything you absolutely didn't do because they weren't there to stop you?"

"No, not at all. We didn't play loud music and run around playing tennis in the house. That would be absurd." He grinned and sipped his drink.

"Of course...absolutely preposterous."

"You're getting the hang of regal charm. I think you could fool a few people into thinking you have always been noble."

"Sounds like fun."

"Precisely." He looked around the room, then took my arm. "Here. Why don't we sit at the top of the stairs and put on a show. Grab you a nice tall glass of wine to sip from. Sit straight and proper. Laugh and chatter about whatever and see who walks up. You have been with Lorena for some time now. I'm sure many people will be intrigued to get acquainted with the new face at the party."

"Where did Lorena go?"

"I'm not sure. Perhaps she went to discuss business. I thought I saw Miss Thaws here somewhere. No matter. She'll find us when she's finished. Now, remember to act just as fancy and self-entitled as everyone else here."

"I'll try."

"Ah, looks like Ms. Thikro is walking by. Say something about the new wine." He sat back and smiled.

Okay, say something intelligent...or something business-related? Should I talk more like the Botligs or Miss Evarchest? Hmm... "Our new product is quite rare. We plan on keeping it that way so we can spend more time ensuring that each batch is flawless."

Emile winked, then turned toward Ms. Thikro. "Good evening. I hope you are enjoying the festivities."

"I am," she responded. "Who is this young lady you are speaking with?"

"Eleanora Wintello, Lorena's new partner. I'm sure you've heard."

"I have heard, though I do not know much of the Wintello family."

"They made quite the wine. A rare find these days. Value is going to skyrocket."

"Really?"

"Of course, she was exceptionally well-qualified to begin working with the Mourlonets. Lorena saw her skill and knew she would be a fine fit for a partner. Swept her up before I could get a chance to."

Ms. Thikro turned toward me. "You seem quite the interest."

How do I respond to that? Say something clever? Compliment? Thank you? This is hard. "Interesting enough to spark the attention of fine nobles. Emile is a wonderful friend and business partner, and I couldn't be happier having an opportunity to be with Lorena."

"Emile does have a good judge of character."

He raised his glass. "That I do."

"I should go find where my husband wandered off to. Pleasant to meet you, Miss Wintello."

Emile watched her walk away, then turned toward me and grinned. "Perfect. She didn't suspect a thing. You pass as a noble quite well."

"I was so nervous. I wanted to be proper but not rude."

"You did great. Honestly people here are much more predictable than you might think. Pick one of five topics: business, economics, skills, profits, maybe some gossip, and they'll be interested. Just sass your way through every conversation and you'll be fine."

"Do people just not know of common families?"

"At this party, no. Most people here don't pay attention to common folk. I wouldn't expect any of them to actually look into the specifics of your past. They will assume you're noble simply because you are with a Mourlonet."

"What if the Botligs tell people about it?"

"They didn't know much about you, just that you started working with the family. You should be fine. Even if these pompous fools find out, they won't do anything about it. Most of them are a bit afraid of Lorena. Quiet, intelligent, and from an extremely powerful family."

"Do you think anyone here knew about Lucian and Lucinda?"

"There were rumors, mainly because he wasn't as quiet about it as he thought, though no one was certain. I don't think anyone would have been shocked. There are always rumors about nobles having affairs with the people they work with."

Looks like Lorena is coming back. "Hello, love."

She sat next to me. "Having fun, dear?"

"A great deal of it," I said, trying to sound fancy.

"Where had you snuck off to?" Emile asked her.

She lifted a small black binder. "Lady Augusta wanted to show me a few new musical pieces she picked up during her travels."

"It has been quite a while since I've heard you play. What was that piece you played for your mother's birthday? That was quite lovely."

"'Autumn Cinders.'"

"You wrote it, correct?"

"Lucian was the primary composer."

"A work of quality, truly. One of my favorite pieces."

"Have I heard it?" I asked.

"No," she responded. "I can play it for you when we get home."

Emile stood up and stretched his arms. "Well, I'm all spent for the evening. Take the car or the coach today?"

I stood next to him. "The coach. Care to escort us out?"

"Gladly." He looped his arm with mine. More people smiled and nodded to me as we left.

Seems our false nobility scandal is working. Viv would love this.

"Until next time, my dears." He nodded and closed the carriage door.

Lorena scooted closer. "All this new confidence. You even fooled the Vintmarkels. I heard them chatting about your family's rare wine."

"Emile led most of the conversation, to be fair."

"I'm glad you enjoyed it."

"I would have even more if you were with me."

"I'm here now." She wrapped her arm around me and pulled me in for a kiss, at least that's how it started. Our hands did admittedly wander…a bit… I might have spent most of that ride on top of her.

I just knew Lucinda was going to find out somehow and tease me about it later.

-

"I take it Worcard's mother isn't thrilled about us," I said, stepping into the entry hall. "She gave me an unpleased look when we walked by."

Lorena handed her coat to Mary Ann. "They spoke with me earlier. She made constant remarks about her son being an exceptional suitor and complained about our generation's lack of tradition."

"Did he say anything?"

"He apologized when she went to get another glass of champagne. He has no personal problem with us."

"Good."

She took my hand and led me back to the music hall. "Most noble families do tend to have more regulations about partners. I imagine Worcard's mother has been pressing him to marry. Sends him to every party hoping he'll bring home a proper woman."

"Were you encouraged similarly?"

"I told my father I had no interest in any of the suitors. I didn't want to spend my life with a man. After that, he no longer invited them to our home. He wished for his children to choose their own paths."

"Something tells me you would have chosen your own anyways."

She smiled. "I would, and I would like you to have the same freedom."

"I like the path I'm on, as long as you are with me."

"Then perhaps..." She got out a simple gold ring and slowly placed it on my finger, looking up at me for approval. "If you would... I know it hasn't been long, but I'm certain about this, and I know people will back off if we are official."

She's... I... We... Oh my. You still have to respond, El...
"Yes." Her lips pressed against mine. Our hands stayed locked together. *We're engaged... ENGAGED... I'm going to marry her. Oh god, I'm getting married...*

Lucinda walked in, immediately seeing the ring. She lit up with excitement. "Joey!"

"What?" Joey responded, peeking her head around the corner.

Lucinda pulled her into the room and wrapped an arm around her. "We have a wedding to plan."

"What?" She looked toward us and smiled. "Oh, congratulations."

Lucinda started pacing around us. "It should be in the spring. Lots of flowers are a must."

"Can we legally officiate it?" I asked.

Lorena smiled. "Even if we can't, to me this is complete. I will always be yours." Her dark brown eyes held genuine care. She handed me a second ring. I was honestly surprised my hands didn't shake as I put it on her finger.

"Mother wouldn't believe it," I said, staring at our matching bands. "She'd take a few days to stop being in denial. She'd just stare at me and say 'Nah,' then go back to washing the dishes. Father had always joked that I should stay single. He didn't talk about it much, but he hated the idea of me and Viv getting married and moving away. He worried about us. Me especially."

"I assume he knew about your preference?" Luce asked.

"Yes, he'd known since I was little."

"Do you have any specifications for your wedding?"

"Vivienne always wanted to be my maid of honor. Aside from that, I didn't really think about it much."

"Let me know if you come up with anything." She pulled out a white sunflower and started laughing.

"What?"

"I just pictured Evangeline as a flower girl, tossing them around like she does in the garden."

Joey laughed. "She'd probably make one of us pick them up right after."

"What music should we have?" Luce asked, spinning around the piano.

I pulled Lorena toward the bench. "You still have to play me that song."

She reached over the keys. Luce and Joey sat down on the stage, listening to the soft tune. It was calm with the occasional flare of higher notes, reminding me of a smoldering campfire, the cinders gently crackling on a cool, fresh evening. The low hum of an owl. A wonder how many adventures you can have by sitting still in front of an instrument.

Chapter 22

"Are you ready, dear?" Lorena asked.

"No. You said there were four?"

"Yes, four."

"No one is prepared for that."

"They aren't that bad. The oldest is Maurice. She's the short, quiet one with long brown hair. Looks the most similar to Evangeline. The second is a taller man, Geralt. He'll spend most of the time rambling about his flower shop. The third is Pat. He'll try to show you pictures of all his children. I'm not sure how many he has at the moment. There were eight, last I heard. Then the fourth is a taller, louder woman. Fit figure. Currently training to be an Olympic swimmer. Her name is Elva."

"Is Eve married?"

"They divorced several years ago. I believe he's a sailor. Still visits her when he's in the area." She handed me my coat and opened the door.

Evangeline is bustling with excitement, rambling about her plans for summer. A little early, but no one's going to try and stop her. Once again, I find myself standing in the garden, completely confused and overwhelmed, though instead of one older deaf lady bossing me around, there are five... Of course she had four children, all equally wild and ragged-looking individuals with enough character to run a theatre. At least they seem to be a happy bunch.

"Great to see you," Elva said, shaking Lorena's hand. "Ma told me you guys had foals. I'd love to see them."

"Of course. They're getting quite big now."

Looks like I'm on my own for a bit. Eve and the taller man—Geralt, I think—are by the greenhouse. The older sister, Maurice, is watering something by the fence, and the younger son, Pat, is kneeling next to one of the flower beds.

Pat waved for me to come over. "Do you know what these sprouts are?" he asked.

"I think we had the...violets here? Something purple..."

"I never really kept up with plants, at least not as much as my siblings."

"I know everything there is to know about grapes, but not flowers."

"Guess we'll have to ask Ma or Geralt... Where did they go?"

"I don't see them. They were here a second ago."

"Those two are always disappearing. Can't think of the last time either of them slowed down or took a day off."

"I'm guessing your mother has always been like this?"

"Yup. Honestly came in handy raising four children. She could always keep track of us. Ran around the house just as much as we did sometimes."

"You wish you had that kind of energy? You do have a lot of children."

216

"Eight, and yes, I really wish I was more like Ma. She comes over sometimes to help entertain them. They love her energy. Gives me and my wife some time to rediscover what it's like to sit down for more than a couple minutes."

"You must be good in crowds, growing up constantly around a bunch of other people."

"I am. Geralt isn't. He gets tired of being around so many people all the time. He used to try and hide in his room and tell us to go away. Me and Elva liked to tease him about that."

"Elva's training for the Olympics, right?"

"She's the best swimmer in the country. I'm sure she'll knock the socks off of the competition when she gets to the big leagues. She gets that from our pa. He used to tell stories about racing his friends from their boat to the shore. Apparently they went a couple years without proper dinghies for their ship, so they had to just jump in at any port that didn't have a deep enough docking area."

"Sounds like he fits right in with the rest of you."

"We are a bunch of characters, aren't we?"

"Wild and free."

He smiled. "We are. What about you, have any siblings?"

"I had a sister. She was killed in the fair stampede a little over a year ago."

"Oh, I'm sorry."

"She was wild as well. Would probably have an easier time keeping up with your mother, to be honest."

"What was her name?"

"Vivienne, though I called her Viv."

"We have our little nicknames as well. I used to call Geralt G, because I knew he hated it, and we all used to call Maurice Rice when we were kids. It was one of the only ways to get her to laugh. She was just as quiet back then."

Evangeline tapped our heads with a long branch. "Dillydallying, are we?"

Pat turned toward her and began signing. "We were waiting for you to get back here and tell us what sprouts these are."

"Those are the violets. Pour the bucket with the old rope handle onto them. That'll get them growing faster than you can talk."

"I talk as fast as you walk, if you can even call it that."

"Boy, you are all full of sass these days."

"We get it from you."

"I'd rather you get this bucket from me and do some work."

"Every visit is a job with you, huh? Can't just take a day to relax. You and Geralt have to race around the garden every time."

"I like to make sure he still knows what he's doing. You and the gals always find ways to fool around."

"I don't know much about plants, Ma. I'm better with kids."

"El, why don't you take him inside to meet Oliver?"

"Okay."

Pat followed me to the door. "He's Lucian's kid, right?"

"Yes."

"Sad he'll never get to meet him. He was a good man. Would have been a fantastic father."

Lucinda sat on the couch with Oliver in her lap. His eyes were glued to the fireplace, mesmerized by the dancing flames.

"Well, look at this fellow," Pat said with a grin. "Cute as ever."

"Hello, Pat," Luce said. "Want to hold him?"

"Absolutely." He reached out and carefully took him from her lap. "He's still pretty young, isn't he?"

"Almost six months."

"Looks healthy, though I'm sure a lad this adorable gets absolutely spoiled here."

"Couldn't be more spoiled."

"Well, he deserves it. He is going to be a lord someday. Lord Oliver Mourlonet. A good, dignified name. I'll have to bring over my younger ones when he's old enough to play. I'm sure he'll like meeting kids close to his age."

"Sounds like a great idea. I don't want him getting too lonely here. He is going to be the only child, at least for a long while."

I sat next to her. "Unless Joey ends up getting serious with Alphonse."

"I'm working on that."

"Now that you're done with me, you're putting all your effort into getting her matched?"

"Is it a crime that I think everyone deserves a good partner?"

"No. If anything, this town needs more hopeless romance."

"Exactly." She smiled and leaned back. "How long are you going to be staying, Pat?"

"Three days," he responded. "Elva has to catch a train back home for her training, and Maurice just got a new job at the docks."

"I'm glad we won't have to help in the garden for a bit. Almost wish we could keep Geralt around. Working with your mother is exhausting."

"I know it. Glad we get to sit in here where its warm, spending time with this little lad."

Oliver returned his eyes to the flames. Quiet and focused.

I wonder what he's thinking, what's stirring through his little mind. He's too young to understand the fire. I guess to him it's just dancing light.

Chapter 23

I walked out of the bathroom. "I'm a little worried about getting this dress dirty. I'm not used to wearing white."

"It's a themed party," Lorena said, adjusting her jewelry.

"Is that why we're overdoing it with extravagance? You never told me what the theme is."

"Contrast."

"Okay, makes sense why you're in black."

She grabbed a shiny silver necklace and put it around my neck. "You're beautiful, my love." She leaned forward to kiss me. "Let's go."

I opened the door. "Lucinda... Right, you gave them the day off."

"They wanted to go shopping for Oliver."

"He grows out of his clothes so fast."

"Mary Ann volunteered to make him some."

"She's so slow he'd grow out of them before he even got to try them on."

"I've never seen her happier."

"She does love kids."

"She's a good teacher."

"Did you ever want kids?"

"I wasn't sure, though now I think one kid in the manor is enough."

"I agree."

Michella stood next to the carriage. "Ready for another extravagant day?"

"You look fancier than usual," I said.

"Just felt like fitting in a little more. I can brag to the other coachmen and drivers."

"Fair."

Back into the carriage. I think I prefer it to the car. It feels fancier, oddly enough. Takes more effort to get the horses ready, shows off not only our handcrafted carriage, but also our finest steeds. The car does look nice, but I guess I have enough memories of grandad's old truck that make them seem plainer. We didn't really use a carriage often, especially one this nice.

"How's the writing going?" Lorena asked.

"Better. I've been focusing mostly on writing little things about my life here. Bavero has been a great inspiration. He is a charming old dog."

"Perhaps you should write one about Dusty Toes."

"Maybe I will."

"He seems to be having an interesting day."

"What do you mean?" I looked out the window, watching the old dog wobble down the street in a nice black suit shirt and tie. *What? Is he...* "Looks like Dusty Toes is ready for the party as well."

"I wonder who managed to get that on him."

"Could have been Luce. She knew we were going to a party today. I wonder if we'll see her walking around."

"She could be anywhere in town, knowing her."

"Probably still trying to set Joey up with Alphonse. She seems so determined to play matchmaker for the whole town."

"She has an eye for romantic potential."

"Odd, the bakery is closed."

"I think Lady Augusta hired them for the evening. She was intrigued by their willingness to try and bake anything."

"I'm sure they're happy for the opportunity. Did I tell you how it went telling them about our engagement?"

"No."

"Ennette practically threw herself at me. Envar immediately started going through different traditional marriage recipes. They are determined to be the bakers for our eventual wedding."

"Hmm."

Wait, did she just give me that look? The 'I'm not telling you something' look. We've been together long enough I know it when I see it.

"Did you sleep well last night, dear?" she asked, staring out the window.

"I did. Had a strange dream where Michella was trying to teach Pete how to do repairs."

She smiled. "Was he good?"

"Excellent, despite his lack of thumbs."

"Pete is not one to let mere thumbs limit his potential."

"Imagine if he had them."

"I'd imagine he would be an astonishing person if he was human."

"Evangeline would still have more energy."

"They would be even fiercer competitors."

"Michella hopefully wouldn't still threaten to cook him all the time..."

She laughed. "No, she would probably threaten to make him be nice to Eve."

"A deaf gardener and a crazy, intelligent goat. Might make a good story."

"I'm sure it would."

Michella stopped the carriage by the door. "I'll have it parked to the side as usual."

"Thank you, Michella," Lorena said, stepping out.

We walked up the steps into the entry hall. Lady Augusta stood on the stairs in a brightly colored blue dress with golden jewels down the front and large golden earrings. Her wrist was adorned in equally shiny jewelry. "Two of the most stunning women I know," she said, walking down to greet us.

Where is everyone? Normally guests are all over the manor. I guess we're early, or they are having a smaller celebration in the ballroom. Seems to be where we're going.

"Right this way." Augusta opened the ballroom doors.

What...? I know all these people... Michella, in a suit? Evarchest, of course still holding documents. Eve, Emile, the Phils, Anthony, Gerome, and Dottie. Luce, Joey, Mary... Everyone's here?

"You look great," Anthony said, walking up in a dark magenta suit.

"Not used to seeing you all fancy."

He smiled. "Didn't know I could be this handsome, did you?"

"Gerome doesn't seem too excited about being dressed up."

"I'm surprised he hasn't spilled wine all over his suit yet."

"Dottie probably threatened him."

"Damn, if Dottie threatened me, I'd listen."

Lorena led me farther in. *Something suspicious is going on...* The room was filled with soft pink roses and candles, complementing white fabrics with gold trim. A smaller table sat near the back with a stack of crème-filled puffs with caramel swirled on top. *Croquembouche. Isn't that for...?*

"You both look stunning," Emile said, walking up.

"Thank you. I wasn't really expecting this crowd."

"Far better company today than our usual business parties."

"Yes..."

"What paperwork is that woman carrying around?"

I looked over to Miss Evarchest. "No idea. She's always carrying something. I wouldn't be surprised if she even sleeps with documents in her hands."

Mary Ann smiled. "She does."

"Really?"

"Yes."

There's Luce, over by the window. Oliver looks so cute in his little suit. Of course he's holding a sunflower. "Luce, Oliver."

"El."

"Decided to spend your day off dressing up?"

Her eyes widened. "I like turning heads..."

"Joey doesn't."

"But she does look cute. Took me forever to get her ready. She'd never put on makeup before."

"How early did you get up?"

"Seven, as usual. We got ready here to not ruin—" She quickly took a long drink from her glass.

"Ruin what?"

"This wine is phenomenal. Of course, you helped make it."

"Luce...? Even Eve is here, and she never leaves the manor."

"See anything interesting on your way over?"

"Were you the one who dressed up Dusty Toes?"

"Mom wanted to stop by town to feed her cats. I got the brilliant idea, ran over to Beatriz's shop, grabbed what I could, she loved the idea, even helped get the suit on him."

"You are being *extra* extra today."

"Thank you."

"Why?"

"Oh look..." She grabbed my arm and led me to the center of the room, stopping me next to Lorena. "I did say I'd start planning it for you," she whispered before walking away.

Oh my...this is actually...

Augusta raised a glass. "To the Mourlonets and the Wintellos. May they find eternal happiness in their union." She lowered her glass. "Any objections?" The room was silent. "Perfect." She brought mine and Lorena's hands together.

Lorena smiled. "I am eternally yours, my love. No matter the puzzle, the challenge, or the storm."

I stared into her eyes. *What do I say? Right, Luce helped me plan this. I wonder if she helped Lorena plan hers as well. Focus, El. You're getting married right now.* "And I am forever yours. Through every place, every obstacle, I will follow you." *Lucinda's handing us the rings. Don't shake, calm down, don't be nervous... I'm sure Lorena will give one of her philosophical speeches on our way home. Something about finding love when you need it. The complexities of emotions.*

Augusta lifted our hands. "May the joy that unites you last forever."

Lorena stepped forward to kiss me. *This is perfect. All our friends are here, we're married... We're married... Viv, I just married the woman I love. Kissed her in front of a crowd. I'm sure you'd be beaming at me if you were here.*

We stepped down off the platform. Miss Evarchest walked up and handed us a marriage certificate and a pen. "Sign these."

I stared at the page in front of me with disbelief. My hand hovered over the document. Lady Augusta had already signed it as an officiate, and Evarchest and Emile signed as witnesses. I tried making my signature fancy, though it didn't quite compare to everyone else's.

Music filled the ballroom. People began pairing off to dance. Lucinda dragged Joey into the center of the room, dancing energetically around her. Emile stood near the back, gossiping with Mary Ann. Ennette and Envar were by the refreshment tables, telling Miss Evarchest about the collection of desserts they made. Bartren stood tall at the end of the table, holding two glasses. *Of course.* Evangeline was walking around, messing with all the plants. Michella followed her, trying to get her to stop and join the party. I couldn't help but smile.

My family... I can't believe how things have turned out. It's been so long since I've seen them, Mom, Dad, Vivienne... I'm married now, part of a noble winemaking family. I wonder what Rodger thinks of all this. I wonder if he knew I'd get along so well here... Wait, is that him?

He started walking toward me. A light green detailing on his suit caught my eye. *Wintello. Our old suit company. Rodger's family had been friends with mine for generations.*

No surprise he would have one. I remember my grandfather wearing a particular suit at every special occasion. It was handmade by his own grandfather. My nostalgia turned to sadness. *The last Wintello is now a Mourlonet.*

"They would be proud," Rodger said, smiling at me.

"Would they? My uncle married out of the name a few years ago, and now I have as well. I have officially ended the Wintellos."

He handed me a small purple book. "They would. I am certain."

"Thank you." I smiled and opened the little book. *A photo album. Grandfather and his old car. Mother and Father in front of the house. Vivienne and me as kids. The donkeys. Mother staring at the large tray of pastries we brought home the first time. Me and Viv riding our favorite pony, Sir Gideon.* My eyes froze on the last picture. Vivienne and I were in front of the house in our nicest dresses. Father stood behind us, grinning with pride. Mother was next to him, looking a little worried. *The dance...*

"What a night! You can't deny that was fun."

"It was. Thanks for staying with me, Viv."

"Could you believe some of those men? The drunk guy who asked for your hand. I couldn't stop laughing."

"I know. I was there."

"As if I would let any regular Joe marry my sister. You deserve someone better, someone to sweep you off your feet, not drunkenly sway around you, completely lost. We need

more charmers in this town. I bet they all go to those fancy parties at that huge estate. I wish we could attend one of those, then I can find you a better partner."

"Honestly wouldn't be surprised if we do end up attending one, with your determination."

"Just think, people who will drool over us respectively."

"That sounds weird."

"Fine. Polite seduction."

That's not better... *"I don't see you being much for 'polite seduction.'"*

"No...but you would. You'd probably be better at picking up some fancy noble than me. You're calm, polite, and stunning. Far worthy of whichever woman does eventually catch your eye."

"Shh, don't wake them. I don't want to get in trouble for staying out later than agreed."

"Right, right. Goodnight, El."

"Night, Viv."

One week later I was standing on the Mourlonet doorstep, staring at a goat. Ironic.

"Hiding in the corner, are we?" Lady Augusta sat next to me with a large grin and an overly fancy glass of wine with gold flakes embedded in the base.

"Just thinking," I responded.

"About those who couldn't attend?" she asked, glancing at the album.

"Yes."

"Well, I'm sure Lucian would be showing off his son with unending pride. He would finally have the right to tease Lorena back about fooling around with a worker. Lady Lillian would be chatting with me about how proud she is, and I'm sure Percival would be right in front of your parents, putting on his best show, asking questions about your heritage."

I smiled. "Vivienne would be off flirting with whichever single man she came across."

She looked back at the crowd. "A beautiful picture."

"As long as Pete doesn't break in. Honestly wouldn't surprise me at this point. He bit a chunk out of some of Miss Evarchest's papers yesterday as she was leaving the manor. She looked so offended."

"Pete? Is he the stubby brown goat of yours that likes to cause trouble?"

"Yes."

"Still breaking out of the barn?"

"Yes..." I glared at her. "What do you know?"

"Lillian taught him that."

"What?"

"She taught him to open the gate to annoy Percival. She loved to mess with him. He always looked furious at first, but his anger would melt away the moment he saw Lillian's satisfied grin."

"Her horse is just as bad. Jumps the fence and refuses to go through the gate properly."

"Seems she left you with a handful of tricks."

"I just hope Pete doesn't teach the other goats to do it."
He did... Thus beginning The War of Red Sunflowers.

The War of Red Sunflowers

For my sister, Vivienne, my inspiration, my source of adventure, and my guide through life.

He was a goat, a very clever goat. He'd learned the schedule of his caretakers, the loud men in the winery, and the short, energetic woman who kept him out of the flowerbeds. He knew some of their names and personalities as well as he knew his own herd. Lillian had been the one to raise him, the one who taught him many more things than his own kind ever could.

The trouble began when he learned to open the gate. He had watched Lillian move the small pieces of metal and would not be deterred by his own lack of thumbs. Every few days or so, he would let himself out. His favorite thing to do was find the stable hand. She would start their game of tag, chasing him around the manor, yelling for him to get back in the barn. It was more fun when she was on horseback. He would race the old grey horse along the fence, darting through the boards when they got too close. He knew every inch of the property, every weakness in the fence, every bush he could hide under.

One day, he would get a chance to escape her. One day he would win.

It was usually a Thursday, though he didn't know that. Michella always took a longer lunch those days, so the gate was left unwatched just long enough. Fresh yellow flowers had just been planted in the garden. He had to have a bite.

He opened the latch and raced toward the flowers. Vast shades of yellows, greens, blues, and warm colors spread across different shapes and patterns, enough to baffle his mind. He reached for a large yellow flower with his teeth, then suddenly felt his hooves rise off the ground. Mud-covered hands tossed him back inside his enclosure. The short lady was always a step ahead of him, standing by the tall yellow flowers with a stern look on her face. He had never learned her name. The other humans never called out to her. Instead, they waved their hands around to get her attention, continuing to move them as they spoke. Something that would always perplex him. Regardless, he was determined to one day get past her. One day he would get a chance to taste every single flower.

It wasn't a Thursday, surprisingly enough. Saturdays were usually too crowded with people to manage an escape, but this particular Saturday was quiet. The people had brought food and cleaned their barn, then left in a hurry. Pete stood by the gate, waiting for his favorite person to show up and tell him to behave, but no one came. The other goats didn't mind. They were happy to munch and dance around their field, but Pete was far too clever to live a simple life. He was obsessed with the humans and their odd words and trinkets and how they created and controlled things with their hands. They knew how the world worked and he wanted to learn more.

Today though, no one was there. Not a single figure. No movement in the garden. No one to stop him this time.

Toast jumped around at his feet, excited to play. She was a scruffy little thing, half the size of her siblings, though with twice the energy. A perfect opportunity, he thought, nudging her toward the gate. *Jump and hit this.*

She wasn't the first he had taught. Others had been smart enough to learn, though none dared leave without him leading the way. They had heard the stories of his childhood, the terrors he faced outside of their fence, the things they couldn't see. He wasn't the leader of the group, but even the elders listened to his words.

The gate swung open. His hooves clamored against the ground, followed by the thunder of fifteen others, all eager to get a taste for themselves. They stopped at the edge where the tall yellow flowers bloomed.

"So, it's war, then." The short lady emerged from the greenhouse, staring with a determined grin. She set down her bucket and wiped her muddy fingers across her face. Pete placed a hoof onto the brick border and let out a loud chuff. The two stood motionless for a few moments, waiting for the other to make the first move.

Poor Toothpick wasn't exactly looking for war. As the smallest and not quite the brightest, he was more inclined to wander and munch, which is exactly what he did, wandered right between the two and reached for a delicious leaf, completely unaware of the tense staring competition he'd just interrupted. Never before had a goat felt such regret. He was immediately swarmed by other goats charging forward, knocking him away from his leaf. He tried and tried for the next several minutes just to get a single bite. Each time he reached, another hoof, plant, or arm would knock him away.

Evangeline had grabbed the first two and quickly tied their legs, leaving them on the path. The third and fourth made a dash for the greenhouse, unaware that the unreasonably clean glass door was in fact closed. Surprisingly enough they didn't make a single crack. All they ended up with were headaches. The fifth, sixth, and seventh ran around her in a circle, hoping to confuse her, that is until Buttercup tripped over a boot and caused a pileup.

Evangeline laughed and pointed to Pete. "Is this the best you've got?"

One by one the others were tackled to the ground, thrashing mud in the air, yelling obscenities that she couldn't understand, not that she could hear in the first place. Pete tried his best to free his friends, but the ropes were taking too much time to chew through. It was eventually down to just him, once again staring face to face with his enemy. A wide satisfied grin was plastered on her face. She grabbed a sunflower, waving it in front of him. His eyes darted to the dark red petals, blurring with fear and confusion. His true nemesis, the color he wasn't supposed to be able to see. The same color that made his friends sick long ago because they couldn't see it. All the wildflowers looked the same to them, and those who ate too much bled the same color.

He was a goat, a very clever goat, and he would not dare challenge the red flowers. Instead, he slowly backed away, helping to drag his friends back to the pasture. Evangeline lifted the flower with triumph, letting out a yell of victory.

Pete froze. Three figures stood by the back door, staring at the scene with shocked expressions. He recognized his favorite human first. She was the only one with bright orange hair. The second was the fancy, dark-haired lady who spent more time with the horses. She was smiling with amusement. The third was the nice newer lady who followed the fancy lady around. He was still figuring out her name. They all wore long, flowing dresses. He knew they must have been out all day, since humans without pants didn't bother with him.

The nice lady waved her hands and spoke. "Uh... Everything alright?"

"Marvelous," the garden lady responded, picking up a goat. "Help me get these trespassers back where they belong."

Michella let out a sigh and approached the nearest goat. The war was over. The stories would be told for generations to come. The garden lady was undefeated. She went out that night and planted red sunflowers around the outer edge of the garden. Neither Pete nor Toothpick ever got a single bite.

-

He went back to his game of tag with his favorite human, occasionally choosing to chase the skinny man instead. He was much louder when he ran, flailing his arms and looking back with fear. He would try to hide behind barrels and vats full of the strange purple liquid. It brought Pete endless amusement.

-

It was once again not a Thursday. Michella was nowhere to be seen. Instead, Joey had fed them that morning and cleaned out their barn before rushing away in a hurry. Once again, Pete stared at the gate, waiting for someone to come and stop him, though no one did. He decided it was time for another adventure. The humans had changed the latch, to no avail. Pete was far too clever to be thwarted by slightly more complex pieces of metal. At the end of the day, it just needed to be moved in the right direction and they were free.

The herd meandered around the property, avoiding the gardens and thorny bushes by the forest. Most took to munching on the grass, lounging in the sun, but Pete didn't move. His eyes were glued to the manor, waiting for the door to open and the chase to begin. Even as the sun slowly set and the others eventually wandered back to the barn for the night, Pete still didn't follow.

A goat in a manor. He didn't think much of it. The door was easy enough to open. There was no grass or hay inside. Instead, there were odd colors, weird patterns, and soft long benches. He wandered around the building, staring at all the shiny objects and weird lights above him, the smooth floors and paintings along the walls.

He turned his head toward the loud chatter of humans. The sound bounced out of a door cracked open in the middle of the hallway. He peeked his head in, listening to their words, hoping to learn something new.

"Wow," he heard Michella say. "Seeing you race across the arena, just trying to hold on, it was priceless, El."

El... Perhaps that was the nice lady's name. He'd heard it before when they talked to each other, but the number of words they spoke made it harder to pinpoint the exact one he was looking for.

"I probably didn't even have to train her," El said.

"Yeah, Bell's smart enough to make her own jumping routine. Which do you think is smarter, your Bell or Pete?"

Pete let out a bleat, happy to be included. The two turned and stared at him in disbelief.

"How the hell did he get in here?" Michella said, setting down her sandwich.

"Wouldn't surprise me if he opened one of the doors and just waltzed in," El responded.

A small, dark-haired human walked into view, staring at Pete with a big smile. He'd seen the boy a few times, usually being carried by one of the taller humans. The boy walked up and pet his head. "Maybe he felt left out. We were gone all day."

Michella sighed and turned toward the door. "I'd better make sure the others aren't out as well. Come on, Pete, back to the barn. I can't get one day off without you making trouble."

"Come on, Pete," the child said, pushing him through the door. "We went to see Aunty El perform in a jumping show. There were so many people, and horses, and little ponies, and a man with a really, really big hat!"

Pete let out a grunt, remembering the time the boy had tried finding a hat that would stay on his head. Hats were unfortunately not made for horned animals, though the boy had persevered and managed to wedge a small top hat between his horns.

"Were you lonely?" the boy asked. "Michella says you get lonely if no one's there to keep an eye on you all day. Maybe we can bring you with next time."

"No," Michella said, opening the barn door. "We can't bring a goat to events, especially one with no respect for gates."

"Oh, okay. Sorry, Pete, I can't take you with me next time." He leaned closer and whispered, "I'll take you on other adventures instead."

From then on, every time the boy was outside, Pete would be with him. Michella wasn't too fond of the idea, but no one could say no to the boy, especially when he asked with wide eyes and a polite smile. Even the frowning woman and her sons were no match. They looked like the dark-haired lady, though older and more energetic. They would visit every so often to talk and glare at everything with judging expressions. Pete had never seen the woman smile, nor speak in a joyful tone. She didn't care for his clever nature or games of tag, though even her unending judgement melted away when the boy approached and said hello. It was a basic greeting, Pete knew that, and perhaps basic was just what was needed. The woman's expression lightened; her eyes showed content. He was the boy who could bring joy to anyone, so Pete would stay by his side to learn the magic of this joy.

-

Pete didn't know where he was going or why the boy had tied him to a small wagon, but he was still happy to go along. Another small human had begun joining them on adventures. She would arrive every few days, accompanied by the skinny wine man that Pete liked to chase. She wasn't nearly as fearful as him. She was smaller and slower and always brought Pete a piece of fruit, which quickly won his approval.

"Where are we going?" the girl asked.

"Somewhere secret. You have to stay quiet," the boy responded.

"Okay."

The three stumbled their way through the forest, following no particular path. Pete's eyes darted around the trees above. The leaves were shifting with color. Some were more yellow than green while others were daker, more dramatic, bringing fear into his eyes and hesitation to his steps.

"What's wrong with Pete?" the girl asked.

"He doesn't like red things." The boy pulled Pete into a small clearing full of tall white sunflowers. "Momma's secret garden. Papa made it for her. They used to have picnics here."

The girl reached out toward the petals. "Wow."

"Momma hides flowers all over the manor, behind paintings, books, the old noisy chair upstairs that no one uses. She has a lot stashed in Papa's room where we sleep."

"Who knows about this place?"

"Just us and Momma." He turned toward Pete. "Don't tell anyone, okay?"

The girl sat down. "So why are we here?"

"I want to put some by Papa's grave. Help me find the smallest ones. We can put them in Pete's wagon."

Pete still didn't know why they were there, or why the small humans were pulling flowers out of the ground and putting them into the wagon, but he was happy to finally get a chance to take a bite. They weren't the best tasting flowers, but at least now he knew. He didn't even get to finish his snack before the boy pulled him back into the trees.

"We have to be quick, Pete. Come on."

He had never ventured past the small stream. There weren't any humans there to bother nor other animals to play with. There was instead a gate. This one was shiny. Far fancier than his, though the thing that baffled him the most was that it had no latch or bar, not a single handle or lock. It was stuck open, covered in thick vines. *Weird*, he thought, *a gate that never closes?*

"You gotta be quiet here, Pete," the boy said, tapping on his nose. "Stay right here."

He didn't mind the dirt being flung onto his back, the laughter of muddied children. He laid next to a strange, tall, rounded stone, listening to the birds. He could feel the eyes of tall humans all around him, though only the children were there. They weren't the best gardeners. The flowers leaned and drooped, dropping petals over the stones.

"Okay, we're done. Let's go." The boy threw the small shovel into the wagon and turned back toward the path.

Pete didn't understand the stones. None had ever been placed for his kind, though the children seemed happy, talking to them like they would one of their own kind. He wondered why the larger humans didn't seem to go there as well... Speaking of... Lucinda was standing by the fence, looking down at the muddied children.

"What were you three up to?" she asked with an unamused smile.

"Nothing..." the little girl said, looking away.

Lucinda reached down into the wagon and pulled out a white petal. Oliver looked at the ground shyly. "I thought Papa would want some, too."

Pete knew she was sad. Humans weren't as easy to read, but he knew the look in their eyes, their shift in tone and breathing. The lady smiled and hugged the boy. "He would..."

Was that it? Did the stones make the larger humans sad? Perhaps that was why they left no trace, no evidence of their visit to the strange gate in the woods.

-

"A goat?"

"He's my assistant," Oliver said, petting the animal's head. "His name is Pete."

The woman adjusted her large circular glasses, staring down at the child. The boy stared back, unwilling to give in to their game of stares. "Very well."

Oliver smiled. "Let's go, Pete. Just like I told you."

Pete had no idea what the boy had told him, nor why this particular lady walked so fast and stared at random objects. Her hands were moving across a clipboard, creating lines and patterns that Pete couldn't understand. Perhaps it was something he could learn if he had hands like theirs. He wished he could ask, though his voice never made the sounds that they did, no matter how hard he tried.

The lady came back every month with a wide smile on her face and a new treat for Pete. The three would walk through the winery and the field of grapes, staring at things and writing notes. Pete had learned to hold a pen in his mouth. He would stare at a bunch of grapes, a flower, or a barrel, then run over to the boy to scribble on his notepad, still with no idea why, but it was nice to be included.

-

The boy got out a crumpled piece of paper. "Aunty told me what all their favorites were. I got everything we need in this bag. We have to get back before it gets dark."

"But it's so far away," the girl said.

"We can take Helena. Michella is on a vacation, so we won't get caught."

"Are you sure?"

"Yes. Let's go."

Pete had no idea how ridiculous he looked sitting on the back of a horse with two small children. He was far too preoccupied with all the strange things he witnessed: the old dusty dog, the group of small children playing on colorful trees, the odd smells floating through the air, and all the wonderous new plants behind the fence. He was tempted to jump down and try them but didn't want to have to try and catch up with Helena after. He was the first to make it beyond the property, beyond the fence, the gate, the garden, and the lady who chased him around. He didn't know where they were going, but no matter the adventure, the distance they traveled, the boy always knew how to get back home.

Again, they approached a tall open gate, just as shiny as the one in the forest. Again, it had no latch or lock, no scrape marks from the ground or dirt on its bars. Another gate that would never close.

The children jumped down and walked up to another strange, rounded stone that jutted out of the ground. Pete sat still on the horse, looking around at all the stones surrounding them. There were far more behind this gate. To him they felt like eyes. Some of the stones were covered in fading flowers, their petals slowly stiffening in the breeze. Again, there were no taller humans in sight, just the birds and the chatter of mischievous children.

"What are you two doing?" An old man wobbled up to them, leaning heavily on a cane. Pete recognized his face.

The girl hid behind the horse. Oliver put down his shovel and walked up to the man. "I thought they would want flowers, like my papa."

The man gestured toward the stones. "He one of them?"

"No, he's buried at home."

"And where might that be?"

"Mourlonet Manor."

The man's eyes widened. A smile crept over his face. "You must be Oliver, then."

"Yes, sir."

"My name is Frolont. I used to work there, in the grape field."

"With Aunty El?"

"Yes, though I got sick... Wasn't acting right and had to leave. How are they doing?"

"Good. Anthony still doesn't let us in the wine building."

"It's no place for children." He looked over at Pete, still sitting on the horse. "Or goats."

"That's what he said."

The man turned toward the girl. "And who might you be?"

"Dahlia... My daddy talks about you sometimes."

"Gerome?"

"Yeah..."

"He still scared of goats?"

"Yeah."

Pete had never heard the man speak so softly. His words were deep and gravelly, slightly strained. He no longer smelled of the strange purple liquid. Instead, he smelled of dirt and flowers.

The man's eyes turned toward the entrance. "Looks like you're about to have company. Can you tell your Aunty El something for me?"

"Okay."

"Je suis désolé."

"I know what that means."

"Good. Learning your home languages is important. You keep out of trouble, now." Frolont wobbled back inside.

The boy sat next to the stone, watching the carriage pull up. Lucinda swung open the door. "Oliver, Dahlia?" She ran up and hugged the boy. "What are you doing out here?"

Oliver turned toward the stones. "They didn't have any flowers. I didn't want them to feel left out."

The woman smiled and turned toward the stones, their stiff grey form now surrounded in soft flowing colors. Two other humans walked up to the stones. The dark-haired lady, and the kind one who was always at her side. She stared at the stones with sadness, and spoke to them as the children did, like she was speaking to another person, just like Pete used to do to the small back door.

He had followed the others through a hole in the fence, out to the forest full of wild plants and endless grass. He had stopped in front of the small red flowers, unwilling to take a bite. They looked funny to him, though the others didn't seem to notice. He remembered the look in his friends' eyes, the blood that dripped from beneath the door. They had all gone through it, and for a while he was alone. He spent his days lying next to it, asking his friends if they were alright. None ever responded. The woman spoke to the stones with the same eyes and was met with the same silence, a silence he understood.

"We should get back. It's getting dark," the dark-haired woman said. "Gerome is going to worry."

Helena was tied to the back of the carriage. Pete found himself being lifted inside. The cushions were far softer than his usual bed of hay. The children sat next to him, staring out the window.

"Don't run off like that. At least take one of us with you."

"Okay, Momma. Did you see the old man?"

"What man?"

"There was an old man there. He said he used to work in the wine building."

"What was his name?"

"Fro... Frot... Lot...something."

"Frolont?"

"Yes. He wanted to tell Aunty El something."

"What?"

"Je suis désolé."

249

Pete didn't know what it meant. He'd heard the humans change their tones and accents. He had learned a few of their words, not realizing how difficult they were making it for him by speaking three different languages whenever they felt. Whatever it meant, it made them smile.

"Was he the one who hurt your hand, Aunty?" the boy asked.

"Yes."

The mother grinned. "So, he actually does know more than swears."

Pete listened. He wanted to know, wanted to learn. So today he would focus, close his eyes, and listen to their sounds.

"I thought you were busy today, Momma."

"You are more important. Besides, I can't just leave Aunty Lorena and El alone in a carriage."

El's face went red. "Cut it out, it was one time."

"Sure it was."

The boy looked up at his mother. "What did they do?"

"Nothing, sweetie, don't worry about it."

"Okay."

Pete was glad to return to his barn and tell of his latest adventure. He told them about the flowers and stones, the strange smells, the old dog, and the gate that never closed. Toast jumped around the barn with excitement, wishing for her own adventures beyond the fence. Perhaps she would one day take over his games and adventures. He understood more than most that he would eventually meet his friends beyond the back door. The humans would live far longer. Someone would need to keep them company, though Toast could not see the red flowers no matter how hard he tried to teach her. So he made a rule. She could let herself out, play among the people, cause all the trouble she wanted, as long as she never ate any flowers outside of their fence.

She didn't know about the door or the blood that covered his friends when he was small, but she would always listen to his words, for he was the goat who could understand the humans.

-

Pete was a goat, a very clever goat. He had once thundered across the field, enjoying a game of tag. He once battled in a glorious war over the gardens. He had been an accomplice to many mischievous schemes and adventures. He had gone beyond the tall fences of his home and seen many strange things. He even once crashed a wedding. Over all his adventures he got to watch the beginning of a young boy's life, the one who taught him words and showed him distant fields. He was no longer afraid of the red sunflowers, perhaps because he could no longer see their vivid colors. His eyes were foggy, his legs were weak, his children and grandchildren had learned to open the gate. He was tired and sore. Now he sat in the garden, next to his favorite boy, happily munching on flowers. The garden lady finally allowed him a victory, to munch as he pleased on the colorful plants. He was a goat, a very happy goat, and the first to get a weird, tall, rounded stone of his own.

"El, dear, are you still in the library?"

"Yes. Just finished my story, Lorena."

"What's this one about?"

"Pete."

"He was a character."

"He was actually the first to greet me when I got here. We had an awkward staring competition on the front porch... It's been ten years... Ten years of making a new home. Ten years since Rodger dropped me off at the manor. Ten years of chasing Pete around, getting dragged around by Luce and Bellezza, watching Oliver grow. Ten years of knowing you"—I grabbed her hand—"mon amour."

"Amore mio."

About the author

Rivara Fall is an author with a passion for peculiar things. Her books fall into several genres including mystery, fantasy, lgbt, sci-fi, and adventure. Born and raised in western Washington, she enjoys rainy weather, playing video games, and spending time with her mischievous pets. Her passions include theatre, science, and art.

If you're interested in seeing her upcoming books, or artistic designs from her stories, you can visit – rivarafall.com

9 798989 929634